I0743329

SWEET DREAMS AT THE FOREVER HOME ON MUDDYPUDDLE LANE

Heart-warming, uplifting romance

Etti Summers

CHAPTER ONE

'**THE ONLY THING NICER** than a custard slice for breakfast,' Nora Bunting announced, picking the gooey treat up with two fingers and lifting it to her mouth. 'Are two custard slices.' She took a huge bite and closed her eyes in bliss.

'You could never eat *two?*' Lori cried, aghast.

'I could,' Nora replied, 'but I won't. And do you know why?'

The youngest member of the hair salon shook her head mutely, bug-eyed with wonder at her boss's prowess when it came to custard slice consumption.

'Because there's only one in the box!' Nora chortled.

'Don't listen to her,' Kendra, the senior stylist, advised. 'Nora's always pulling our legs. She'd never eat two for breakfast. Lunch, maybe, but not breakfast!' She slapped her black-trousered thigh and nudged Nora with a playful elbow.

'Careful,' Nora admonished. 'I nearly dropped my slice.' She finished it in a couple of mouthfuls, then proceeded to try to lick the incredibly sticky icing from her fingers, before resorting to washing her hands in one of the three basins.

 'Right, I suppose we'd better get this show on the road,' she said, taking a gulp of frothy coffee. 'Who've we got this morning?' She turned to Kendra, who opened the appointments book to today's date.

'A full head of foils for Stacey Heron, a restyle, a root touch up, two cut and blow dries, and Mrs Blake's regular wash and set. I think she'll need a trim as well, because her hair was getting a bit bushy last week.'

Nora asked, 'Who's first?'

'The foils and one of the cuts.'

'Can you remember what we need to do for the foils?' Nora asked Lori.

'Um... put a gown on the client?'

Nora loved training the next generation of hairstylists and she was never without a student, but this one was harder work than most. The seventeen-year-old was eager to learn, bless her, but the girl's lack of common sense sometimes amazed her.

'We put gowns on *all* our clients,' Nora reminded her gently. She tried again. 'What equipment do we need?'

A lightbulb came on. '*Oh*, foil strips!'

'That's right. What else?'

'Bowls for the colour and brushes to apply it?'

'Correct. And we also need the customer's record card, so I know what was discussed when she came in for her consultation. Do you think you could get all that ready for me? And when you've finished, you'll need to stock up the towel shelf and make sure all the shampoos and conditioners are topped up. But before you get started, *please* could you make me another coffee?' She yawned. 'This flippin' menopause is a pain in the bum. I keep waking up in the middle of the night for a wee and then I can't get back to sleep.'

'What did the doctor say?' Kendra asked.

'I've got to wait for the results of the blood test first, before he'll give me HRT. At least I'm not suffering from hot flushes yet.' Nora grasped the neckline of her top and pulled it away from her chest, fanning herself. 'Although, now I come to think of it, I *am* rather hot.'

'It's really warm out,' Kendra said. 'The forecast reckons it'll be twenty-five degrees today.'

Nora loved the summer, but preferably when she was lying on a beach with a cocktail in her hand: she didn't want to have to work in it. Even this early in the day, she could feel sweat gathering between her ample breasts and creating damp patches under her arms.

Lori brought her another coffee and Nora gulped it thirstily. She would send the girl out to the shop for a bottle of something cold in a bit. She loved her coffee, but if it was going to be as warm as Kendra claimed, she'd need a cold drink, and preferably one with caffeine in it to keep her awake.

She hoped the doctor would prescribe HRT, because the sooner she got started on it the better. Being tired all the time was getting her down.

The door opened and Stacey Heron, a regular and the salon's first client of the day, came in and soon Nora and her team were immersed in washing, cutting, curling and styling. As Picklewick's only hairdresser, the salon was always busy, and despite being rushed off her feet, Nora loved it. Ever since her college days, she'd wanted to own her own place, and she'd built the business from scratch. Very proud of it she was too, and although she joked and laughed with clients and staff alike, she had high standards and ran a tight ship. Even as she concentrated on wrapping lengths of foil around strands of colour-daubed hair, she kept a close eye on what everyone else was doing, at the same time maintaining a steady stream of chatter with her client.

The current topic of conversation was plans for the weekend.

The woman in the chair was saying, 'If the weather holds up, I'd quite like to have some friends around for a barbeque. We've got one of those inflatable pools, so the kids can play in that while the grownups enjoy a couple of beers. Or in my case, wine.'

'I like a nice cold glass of Pimm's,' Nora said. 'Or a pina colada with loads of ice. A barbeque sounds good – as long as I'm not expected to cook it!'

'God, no! I leave that to my husband. What is it with men and barbeques? If I asked him to shove a burger under the grill in the kitchen, he'd make a right song and dance about it, but ask him to stick a sausage on the barbie and he's there! He's even got a stupid apron that he wears.' Stacey rolled her eyes indulgently. 'I swear a barbeque brings out the caveman in them.'

Nora laughed. She'd witnessed that very thing with her friends' husbands and partners.

Stacey asked, 'What are you doing on the weekend? Something more exciting than eating a burnt burger in the garden surrounded by screaming kids, I bet.'

'I'll be in the salon until two on Saturday, but I'm going to that new tapas bar in Thornbury in the evening, and I'm hoping to have a long lie in on Sunday, followed by lunch at The Black Horse.'

Stacey sighed. 'I envy you. I'd sell my youngest for a lie in. He's seven now, but he still gets me up at six in the morning.'

'Just wait until he's seventeen,' Kendra warned, as she placed a rubber cape around her client's neck prior to re-styling the woman's shoulder length hair. 'He'll sleep in, all right, but you'll still be exhausted because you won't be able to drop off until he gets home. It was gone one o'clock before mine got in last night. And he's got college this morning. I had hell's job to get him out of bed.' All the time she was talking, Kendra was running her fingers through the client's wet hair, checking its length before she took the scissors to it.

Nora joined in, 'And by then you'll probably be menopausal as well, so your sleep will be disturbed anyway!'

'I'm coming back as a bloke next time,' Stacey declared adamantly. 'They don't have problems like periods, or childbirth, or the blasted menopause. I'm not looking forward to that, I can tell you.'

It definitely wasn't a barrel of laughs, Nora thought. 'Right, that's your foils done. I'll put the timer on for thirty minutes, and we'll see how it goes. You might need a bit longer. Can I get you a cup of tea or coffee? A magazine?'

After instructing Lori to make the client a drink, Nora retreated to the back room for a quick swig of the cold cola the girl had fetched for her, and one of the muffins

Kendra had brought in for their elevenses. Okay, so what if it *was* only ten o'clock? She was hungry: the custard slice hadn't touched the sides.

Sinking into the battered office chair to eat it, she was glad to take the weight off her feet. Only another seven hours and she could go home and have a nap. This really was getting ridiculous. She was only forty-seven, yet lately she felt more like *seventy*-seven. Stacey was right, men had it easy when it came to hormones.

Sighing loudly, Nora tucked into the muffin, and she'd just finished washing it down with another swig of fizzy pop when her mobile rang.

It was the surgery.

Yay! The result of her blood test must be in – HRT at last!

'Miss Bunting? It's Dr Watts. I'd like you to make an appointment to see me. It's about your results.' He sounded more sombre than a confirmation that she was well on the way to menopause warranted, and a chill shivered down her spine.

'Sooner rather than later, if you can manage it,' he added, and the chill became an artic blast of dread.

'Oh, no, you can't do this to me. I need to know *now*, not in a week's time or whenever I can get an appointment. Is it...?' She couldn't get the word out, but she was fearing the worst.

'The menopause? Well, yes, your hormone levels do indicate that you're in perimenopause, but I'm more concerned with your HbA1c level.'

'My *what?*'

'I'm sorry to say but your blood glucose is sixty-six.' He paused before uttering the words that would change her life forever. 'You have diabetes.'

ELIJAH GRANT SLID the final tray of lemon crumble muffins into the industrial sized oven, set the timer, then limped slowly over to a high-backed stool beside the work prep table, and eased himself onto it with a wince. His leg ached abominably, but then, he had been on his feet since five-thirty this morning, so even with the boot for support, it was going to hurt.

He hoped the hospital would tell him he could take it off when he went for his appointment at the clinic later today. On the other hand, at least it was a boot and not a plaster cast, so he counted himself lucky he hadn't completely fractured his tibia. A stress fracture, they called it, where the bone was weakened by excessive training or overpronation of the foot whilst running. The first was his own fault – the second could partly be compensated for by the correct footwear.

Elijah glared at the blue boot in distaste. He hated the damned thing and kept taking it off. Although it provided support to the healing bone, he was concerned that his leg was losing muscle mass and strength. And since he was rather slim, he didn't have that much muscle to lose, so he wanted to hang onto what he had.

He'd been tempted to not wear the boot at all today, but he knew he'd regret it if he didn't. He kept telling himself he shouldn't try to run before he could walk, but that's what he was – a long-distance runner. Running is what he did, who he *was*. Okay, he was a baker as *well*, but baking was for paying the bills and giving him something to do when he wasn't running. Running fed his soul, and ever since he'd managed to get a stress fracture and had therefore been unable to run, his soul had been hungry. Starving, in fact.

While he waited for the timer to ding, he checked the RunMad app. It was his favourite thing to do – apart from actually running. The app was his social life and entertainment rolled into one; more so now that he wasn't able to get out and train.

When he wasn't out pounding the streets, he was looking at other people's uploaded routes, times, elevation and distances, or he was watching videos about running, or reading blog posts about running, or drooling over adverts for the latest performance trainers or rehydration drinks. To say he was obsessed was putting it mildly.

The first account he checked was Cameron's, and Elijah was both proud and envious to see that his son had done a twenty-mile training run yesterday in a little under two hours forty-five minutes. He noted it was one minute faster than the last twenty miler Cameron had done.

Marathon running was an endurance sport, and a time-consuming one at that. To run the kind of distances Elijah and Cameron ran, you had to be prepared to put in hours and hours of training.

He clicked on the 'kudos' button, showing Cameron that he was giving him a virtual pat on the back and a thumbs up for his run, and commented, 'Nice one.' Then he scrolled through his feed to see who else had posted runs. Some people (not many), Elijah knew in real life, having taken part in races with them, but most he only knew as a thumbnail photo and a username. Still, that didn't matter. It was the runs they'd done that mattered to him.

After commenting on a few more, he put the phone away, and just in time too, as Andrea, who managed the retail part of the bakery along with supervising the other staff, stuck her head around the door. She was always teasing him for having his phone in his hand, so he was pleased he'd not given her the opportunity.

'We've had another customer ask for spelt flour bread,' she said. 'That's six in the last week. Do you think there might be a market for it?'

'Probably.'

'Can't you give it a go?'

'I suppose I could, but not today. For one thing, I don't have any spelt flour, and for another I'm off to the hospital in an hour. Fracture clinic,' he added. To be honest, he really couldn't be bothered trialling something new, even if there was a call for it. He preferred to spend his time doing what interested him – running, or thinking about running, or watching videos about running...

'Ooh, do you think they'll tell you to leave the boot off?' Andrea asked.

'I hope so!' His reply was heartfelt. 'I'm already going to miss one marathon; I don't want to miss any more. And Cameron and I are supposed to be training for the Marathon des Sables.'

'I thought you said it wasn't until next year?'

'It's not, but it's a beast. It isn't called the toughest foot race on earth for nothing!' he enthused, warming to his theme even though he'd told her all this before. 'Six marathons over six days, in desert temperatures of over 40° Celsius,' he continued. It gave him goosebumps just thinking about it. It would be the hardest challenge of his life and he'd be running it with his son. He couldn't wait!

Andrea shook her head. 'There's something wrong with you. How anyone can call that fun is beyond me. I hope, for all our sakes, that they *do* take your boot off, then perhaps you won't be so miserable.'

'I'm not miserable,' Elijah protested.

She gave him a pointed look. 'Yes, you are. Do you want me to see if the muffins are done?' she asked, and he realised the timer had gone off.

'I'll do it.' He'd given his leg a bit of a rest, so it was time he used it again. It wasn't going to get stronger by molly coddling it. He needed to use it as much as possible.

Gritting his teeth, he got off the stool and hobbled to the oven. The muffins looked absolutely delicious, and in the interests of making sure they tasted as good as they looked, he broke a piece off and popped it in his mouth, offering the other half to Andrea.

'Not for me, thanks. If I tasted everything you baked, I'd never eat any proper food.'

'Are you saying my baking isn't proper food?' he asked, putting the other half in his mouth and chewing appreciatively.

'You know what I mean,' she scolded. 'It's alright for you, you're as skinny as a whippet.'

'That's because I exercise a lot.'

'Yes, well, some of us don't have time to go running for three or four hours a day, seven days a week.'

'Four days,' he corrected. 'I don't exercise *seven* days a week.'

She put her hands on her hips. 'You go for a "jog", but not a normal jog. People *jog* around the park. *Your* version of a jog is to go to Thornbury and back. That's nine miles each way. As I said, you're not normal.' She huffed out of the room, and his rueful smile followed her.

Maybe he did take his running a smidge too seriously, but he enjoyed it. It got him out of the house, gave him exercise, and kept him fit. And compared to other hobbies, like golf, for instance, it was relatively cheap. All it cost him was a new pair of trainers every few months, and he usually bought those whenever the sports shop had a sale on.

Elijah put the muffins to cool, then checked the time. He needed to make a move if he didn't want to be late for his appointment at the clinic.

ELIJAH SAT IN THE waiting room tapping his feet. Correction: tapping his foot. The one *without* the boot. The fractured one was aching like the devil, so he was keen not to move it too much.

When he heard his name called, he levered himself up with the crutches that he'd been given but hated using. For one thing, he didn't want to get told off for not using them, not with being so close to being able to leave his boot off completely, and two, because he didn't think he could reach the consulting room without them.

The nurse slowed down to allow him to catch up. 'It looks a lovely day out there,' she said conversationally.

'It is, and I hope it'll be a lovely day in *here*.' He pointed to his boot. 'I'm hoping this will come off.'

She opened a door to a small room containing a desk, a computer, and a woman sitting at it studying the screen.

'Mr Grant?' the doctor said.

'Call me Elijah.'

'Okay, Elijah, I'm just going to run through a couple of checks to make sure we've got the right person, then we'll see what's what, okay?'

Impatient to get on with it, Elijah rattled through the answers.

Satisfied, the doctor told him, 'I'm pleased to say the fracture has healed nicely.'

'Does that mean I can take this off?' He was beaming.

'You may.'

'Thank the Lord for that!'

'I'll arrange for some physio for you, to help strengthen the muscles around—'

'No need, doctor. I know the exercises I have to do.'

'Ah, yes, this is the second tibial stress fracture you've had on this leg, isn't it? It says in your notes that you're a marathon runner.'

'That's me – I run marathons. I've managed to get into the Marathon de Sable next year. Me and my son.'

She looked at him blankly, so he went on to explain what it was, ending with, 'I can't wait to start running again.'

'How often do you train? And for how long?'

'Four or five times a week for the longer distances, and in between, I do shorter runs, around fifteen or twenty miles.'

'That's a *shorter run?*' Her expression was incredulous.

'Of course, I know I'll have to take it easy for a bit, and—'

'Mr Grant – Elijah – I don't think you understand. This is the *second* stress fracture you've had on this leg. If you continue with the same level of activity, there will be more. I am strongly advising you to hang up your trainers for fear of doing yourself permanent damage.'

Elijah gawked at her, stunned, unable to believe what he was hearing. 'Could you say that again?' he stammered.

The doctor's face was sympathetic, but her tone brooked no argument as she told him in no uncertain terms, 'I'm sorry, but you'll have to accept that your running days are over.'

CHAPTER TWO

'I'M GOING TO DIE,' Nora wailed, sniffling into a tattered tissue.

Trinette picked up a plate of biscuits and held it out to her. 'Not just yet, surely?'

Nora took one and bit into it, crumbs cascading down her cleavage. With her mouth full, she replied, 'No, but I could go blind or lose a leg.'

'Did the doctor actually *say* that?' her bezzie wanted to know.

'Uh huh.' Nora nodded. 'He said it's a serious condition and I need to take it seriously.'

'Seriously?'

'Yep.' What scared her the most – as if the threat of going blind or having a foot amputated wasn't scary enough – was that he'd wanted to see her as soon as possible. Like, *today*. He said he could fit her in this afternoon and GPs *never* did that. Getting an appointment was normally as hard as catching smoke with your bare hands. She'd had to wait ages the last time, yet miraculously he'd been able to see her *this afternoon?!*

Nora had struggled on with her work in the salon until the time of her appointment, trying her best to pretend nothing had happened, but inside she'd been reeling. *Diabetes.* Wasn't that a disease old people got?

Every chance she had, she'd reached for her phone and googled it, but she'd only ended up scaring herself even more. And now here she was, sitting in her bezzie's lounge and crying on her shoulder.

'I didn't know he was even testing me for diabetes,' she added tearfully. 'My gran always used to say she hated going to hospital because you went in for one thing and came out with another – usually worse than the very thing you went in for! I always thought she was joking. I wish I hadn't gone to see him now – I only wanted HRT.'

'Did he prescribe you any?'

'No. He was more concerned about my blood sugar level, my cholesterol, and my blood pressure. They're all too high.'

'Did he give you *anything?*'

'Advice.' Nora spat out the word. 'Lose weight, was the main one. Oh, and he gave me a couple of leaflets.' She fished them out of her bag and glanced at them helplessly. 'He said he's going to give me a chance to bring down my HABC, or whatever the hell it's called, and test me again in three months.'

'But can't they give you anything for it?'

'They *can*, but he doesn't want to. He said that putting a patient on medication doesn't address the root cause.'

'Which is?' Trinny was looking as concerned as Nora felt.

'Diabetes is sometimes genetic and there are other reasons, but in my case he thinks it's mostly due to bad diet, not enough exercise, and too much visceral fat.' Nora grasped the rolls of flesh bulging over the waistband of her work trousers and jiggled them.

Trinette gasped. 'That's fat shaming! You ought to report him. What has he got against curvy women, that's what I'd like to know!' Trinny wasn't a skinny waif, either.

Nora wished it was simply a dislike of cuddlier ladies that had driven the doctor to tell her to lose weight, but she feared it wasn't. From the snippets she'd gleaned from the internet, she had a feeling he might be right.

'What about your menopause symptoms, the waking in the night, the tiredness? What's he going to do about *that?*' Trinny demanded.

'Um, he says it's the diabetes that's making me feel this way.' Apparently, being constantly thirsty, weeing a lot (especially at night), and feeling knackered all the time were classic symptoms.

'What are you going to do?'

Nora let out a resigned sigh. 'I supposed I'd better try to lose some weight.'

To be honest, she didn't know where to start. She'd never dieted in her life, and she'd never wanted to. She was happy with her body and had never desired to be slim. She also liked food too much to restrict what she ate. And by food, she didn't mean stuff like salads, either. The food she liked was hearty and substantial. Food such as pies and stews, casseroles and hot pots, pasta, pizza, chips, cakes... *Real* food. not rabbit food.

'You could try going to the slimming club in the community centre?' Trinette suggested, but Nora shuddered.

The thought of a public weigh-in was just as abhorrent to her as a public hanging. Anyway, she'd already been weighed at the surgery, and she hadn't enjoyed the experience in the slightest.

Three stone overweight.

Who knew?

Obviously not her. She'd suspected she was a little on the heavy side, but not *three stone*. And according to the GP, a three stone loss would only just put her at the top end of the ideal weight range for her five feet five-inch height. If she wanted to be in the middle, she needed to lose four stone in total. *Four!*

That wasn't going to happen, was it?

'Aw, hun, I'm sure it's not as bad as he made out,' Trinny said, offering her another biscuit, which Nora took. 'I mean, lots of people have diabetes and they're okay.'

Unfortunately, Nora suspected it *was* as bad and that she might never be okay again.

'**ARE YOU ALRIGHT?**' Andrea asked Nora the following morning when she popped into the bakery for her usual cakey breakfast. 'You look a bit tired.'

 A *bit* tired? Nora suspected Andrea was being polite. When she'd got ready for work this morning, her mirror had practically recoiled at the sight of her pale, drawn face and dark-circled eyes. And she laid her lack of sleep last night firmly at diabetes's door; she hadn't slept a wink because she'd been reading anything and everything on the subject that she could get her hands on. Starting with the leaflets the doctor had given her, then swiftly moving on to the internet, she'd devoured every morsel of information, swallowing some of it and spitting out other bits until her brain was so full she thought her head might explode. It was bursting at the seams with facts and figures, dos and don'ts, but the general consensus of all the websites and forums was that carbs and sugar were out and healthy eating and exercise were in.

It made her want to weep. In fact, she did have another cry, along with a hefty portion of 'why me?' and a side order of self-loathing. If she'd paid more attention to her diet and had more self-control when it came to bread, cakes, biscuits, sweets, chocolate, crisps – the list could go on – maybe she wouldn't be in a situation where she'd have to watch what she ate forever. Diabetes, she'd discovered to her sorrow, was for life. It wasn't going to go away; she was never going to be cured, no matter how much weight she lost nor how much exercise she did. She could never go back to her normal way of eating, nor her normal lifestyle, because that was what had got her into this pickle in the first place – and *why* was her every thought *food-related*?

'Nora?'

'Huh? Oh, sorry, I was miles away,' she said, realising Andrea was waiting for a response. Or hoping she wasn't about to keel over. 'Busy, that's all. I've got a lot on my mind,' she added.

Abruptly she felt a blush whoosh up her chest and into her face. What was she doing in the bakers when this was supposed to be the first day of the rest of her non-baked-goods life?

Grabbing the neckline of her top, she fanned herself rapidly.

'Hot flush?' Andrea sympathised. 'I get them all the time. The damned menopause is a damned nuisance!'

Wordlessly, Nora nodded. It wasn't strictly a lie – she did have hot flushes – but this one was caused by shame, not the menopause.

She couldn't help feeling that if she confessed to being diabetic, people would look at her generous curves and come to the conclusion that she'd brought it on herself. Hell, why wouldn't they, since she was thinking the exact same thing? It wasn't fair, though; there were loads of overweight people who didn't have diabetes (Trinny, for one), and Nora felt she'd been dealt an unlucky hand. After all, she didn't sit on her backside all day stuffing her face with cake. She had an active job and was on her feet from nine in the morning until seven in the evening some days. Okay, one day: Thursday was late night opening. And Saturday was early closing. And the salon wasn't open on Sundays. But the rest of the time she was on her feet because you couldn't cut hair sitting down. Well... you *could,* and you *should* if the client had long hair, but the vast majority of the time hair cutting was an activity best performed standing up.

Andrea asked, 'What can I get you today? A coffee puff? A custard slice? Or how about a nice Belgian bun?'

'Actually, I don't think I'll have a cake,' Nora found herself saying. 'Just three chocolate chip cookies, please.'

Start as you mean to go on, she thought. And she meant to go on by cutting *down*, not cutting *out*. She'd still have her treats, just not as many or as often. Or as much. One slice of cake instead of two, for instance. And swap normal pop for the zero sugar variety. Maybe invest in some reduced sugar syrup for her coffee, too. Going cold turkey wasn't for her – she'd never be able to stick to it.

Until something happened later that day which made her realise that she might not have any choice...

'IT'S A LOVELY DAY, so why does everyone look so miserable?' Andrea wanted to know as Elijah limped into the shop with a tray of twisted blueberry buns fresh from the oven. Still warm, they smelt divine, but he barely noticed.

Andrea was saying, 'First there was the postie, because his van had a flat tyre. Ashton, I said to him, at least it's not raining. Then there was Nora from the hairdressers. She looked washed out, poor thing. But the menopause can do that and I think she's suffering a bit. I couldn't even tempt her with a custard slice. So,' she put her hands on her hips, 'what's your reason for having a face like a slapped arse? Is your leg hurting? I see you're not wearing your boot. Did they tell you to take it off?'

'Yeah.' Elijah didn't want to say any more. He couldn't. If he did, he feared he might howl.

'You do look a bit pale and drawn. Why don't you sit down for a bit? Have you taken any painkillers?'

It wasn't his leg that was aching. It was his soul. No more running? Elijah couldn't contemplate life without it.

And how was he going to tell his son?

Abruptly Elijah felt old, worn out, on the scrapheap. He'd envisioned himself still running into his seventies and eighties, yet at fifty-two he was washed up. He hadn't believed the doctor. Had asked for a second opinion. And when she'd gone to see whether the consultant was available, he'd been convinced she was wrong.

But she hadn't been. And Elijah was devastated. What was he supposed to do now?

Last night he'd lain awake, telling himself he should be grateful for what he had. There were people who were in far, far worse situations than him, unimaginably worse. He had his health, he owned his own business, he owned his own house; he even had all his own teeth and a full head of hair (although it was receding ever so slightly at the temples). But nothing could console him. His life was about to undergo a major upheaval, and he wasn't ready for it.

Was he overreacting?

He suspected he might be. His ex-wife would probably tell him to get over himself. Get a grip. Find another hobby. But running was what he *did*. It was who he was, and he didn't think he had it in him to reinvent himself.

And then there was his son. Running was what connected him and Cameron. Was that about to be lost? Cameron was twenty-two, with a promising career and a busy social life. Would Elijah see as much of him if they didn't go running together? Would his son now regard him not as a fit, agile man who happened to be his dad, but as a middle-aged boring person who he had to visit out of duty once or twice a month?

Elijah hated to admit it, but there was also a sense of pride in being a long-distance athlete at his age. Most of the guys he'd been in school with had beer bellies and man-boobs, and on the odd occasion when he bumped into one of them, he was secretly pleased with how he measured up.

No longer being able to run was unthinkable. Yet that's what was happening. *Had* happened. He'd run his last marathon.

The question he now had to ask himself was, what could he do instead?

NORA SQUINTED CROSSLY at the appointment book. The pencilled in details were blurry, so she took off her reading glasses (she'd reached the age where she, along with many of her contemporaries, were forced to wear them), and blew on them to create a momentary fine coating of mist on the lenses, then gave them a rub with the hem of her tabard.

Replacing them on her nose, she peered at the diary again.

Annoyingly, the writing was *still* blurry, so she took the glasses off once more and held them up to the light. Both lenses looked clean enough, but she gave them another polish anyway.

It was only when she popped them on again, did she realise it wasn't her glasses that were the problem – it was her *eyes*. Her right eye, to be exact.

Nora went hot, then cold, as nausea swept over her. With a racing heart and clammy hands, she picked up her phone and did a quick google search. Squinting through her good eye, she confirmed her fears: blurred eyesight could be a sign of high blood glucose, and as she'd discovered during her research last night, high blood glucose could lead to impaired vision, even blindness.

Oh, hell.

CHAPTER THREE

NORA CLUTCHED THE shopping list in her hand as she wandered up and down the supermarket aisles. Her cupboards, fridge and freezer were woefully bare of anything edible (and by edible, she meant *tasty*) because in a state of panic last night she'd thrown out everything with even a hint of carbs or sugar. Which hadn't left a lot: her fridge had only milk and butter in it, and a sorry-looking iceberg lettuce, and the cupboards held little more than a jar of Marmite, three eggs and a small bottle of brown vinegar – and she was having second thoughts about the vinegar.

The thought of what *wasn't* in her freezer made her want to weep – the bag of frozen broccoli didn't have the same appeal as the tub of salted caramel ice cream she'd binned. If it hadn't already thawed to a runny gloop, she might have been tempted to fish it back out last night and have it for supper.

After her frantic emergency appointment with the optician this morning (thankfully her vision had sorted itself out overnight, but she went anyway, in case it happened again), she'd not gone into work for the final hour. Instead, she'd come to the supermarket in Thornbury, even though she'd felt as guilty as sin for leaving her staff in the lurch, despite the salon closing early on Saturdays. Kendra had been fine about it, but still, Nora hated to impose. The salon was *her* business, *her* responsibility, and taking time off went against the grain. However, she'd been realistic enough to realise that she wasn't in the correct frame of mind to trim a hedge, let alone a client's hair, so it was better all round if she stayed away.

Unfortunately, Nora wasn't in the mood for grocery shopping either, since she could no longer linger over the selection of biscuits or creamy desserts such as chocolate mousse. But it had to be done if she wanted to eat, which she most certainly did. She was starving: two hard-boiled eggs had been all she'd managed to force down today, and to be fair, even if she'd been hungry at breakfast, there hadn't been much to choose from since she'd thrown almost everything else away. Wasteful, she knew, but considering she couldn't eat it, what else was she supposed to do with it? Besides, she typically did her weekly food shop on a

Saturday anyway, so her kitchen wasn't as well stocked as it otherwise might have been.

Nora eyed the contents of her trolley with dismay. So far, it contained an abundance of leafy green vegetables, salad stuff, and berries. Oh, and two sets of weighing scales: one for the kitchen and one for the bathroom, because *apparently* she was going to become one of those people who weighed herself and her food. Oh, and she was also going to be studying the back of everything she bought to check the carb content.

Deep joy.

She was going to be a bundle of laughs on a night out, wasn't she?

Nora gasped and clapped a hand to her mouth. Would she be able to have a *drink?* She loved a glass of wine or a cocktail, but how would alcohol affect her blood glucose? In fact, how would *anything* she ate or drank affect it? Because she wasn't on medication (not yet anyway, and hopefully she wouldn't be), she hadn't been provided a way to monitor her glucose levels. Apparently, that's what some diabetics, especially those on insulin, had to do.

Oh, heck, there was so much she didn't know and such a lot of conflicting advice out there, that she had no idea which way to turn. There were a few things everyone seemed to agree on though, and the main one was losing weight, but regular exercise and reducing carbs also featured heavily.

Suddenly Nora felt like crying, and her eyes brimmed with unshed tears and her chin wobbled.

'Are you alright, lovie?' an elderly lady asked, peering at her with concern.

Nora pressed her lips together and sniffed loudly before she gained enough control to say, 'I don't know.'

'Is it a man?'

That made Nora smile in a wobbly, watery way as she shook her head. 'I've never cried over a man in my life. Well, not since Barney Giles in Year Eleven, but I was only fifteen at the time.'

'Had some bad news?' the woman persisted.

It really wasn't any of her business and Nora had no idea why she told her, but she found herself blurting, 'I've just been told I've got diabetes.'

'Type 1 or Type 2?'

'Uh, Type 2, I believe.'

'What are your numbers?'

'My what?'

'Your HbA1c, your blood glucose level.'

'Er, sixty-six, I think the doctor said.'

'That's not too bad. Forty-one and under is considered normal, but you can get it down.'

'So I believe.' She glanced at the trolley and pulled a face. 'I'm not looking forward to it. It's a complete change of lifestyle.'

'It is, but you can do it. Look at me, I'm seventy-six. I've been diabetic for over thirty years and I'm still here. Watching what you eat becomes second nature after a while. I've got one word of advice for you – distraction. Whenever you feel like raiding the biscuit tin or shoving the contents of the fridge in your mouth, drink a large glass of water and go *do* something. Clean the oven, paint the bathroom, do twenty laps of the living room, take the dog for a walk.' The woman patted her on the arm. 'Heed my advice and you'll be in remission in no time. Good luck, dearie.'

Nora, mouth open in bemusement, watched her toddle off down the dairy aisle. Clean the oven, indeed? Huh! And neither was she going to paint the bathroom (she didn't do DIY), do laps of the living room (it was a decent sized room, but not big enough to do *laps* around), or take the dog for a walk, because she didn't have one.

There must be *something* she could do, she mused as she followed the old woman towards the cheese selection, but right now, she had no idea what.

NORA WAS CURRENTLY eating a late lunch whilst trying to think what form of exercise she could do. Swimming? Uh, no. It would ruin her hair.

Go to the gym? she grimaced. She'd never been one for pounding away on a treadmill or getting a sore backside from sitting on a pedal machine.

Staring into space, her eyes narrowed as she went through her options, she tried not to think about the chicken salad she was ploughing her way through. The chicken part was quite nice – she'd grilled it with some seasoning out of a jar that she'd sprinkled over it. It was the salad part she was struggling with. Talk about uninspiring! And her jaw ached from all the chewing and crunching she was having to do. It was worse than eating nut brittle toffee.

Oh, don't, she groaned silently. It was best not to think about forbidden delights such as *toffee.*

Depressed, she shovelled another forkful of mixed salad leaves into her mouth and munched despondently as her thoughts returned to the problem of exercise.

How about outdoor cycling as opposed to cycling in the gym, she debated, then wrinkled her nose. Not only would she have to buy a bike, she'd have to be prepared to go out in all weathers, and she knew what she was like. She was lazy when it came to exercise. If she lived far enough away from the salon to warrant cycling to it, that might be an incentive, but it only took her seven minutes to walk to work.

Jogging? Nora pulled a face. Not with *her* boobs and backside. To even consider jogging, she'd have to lose weight first, which was somewhat of a catch-22 situation.

Aerobic classes? Hmm, that was a possibility, but she couldn't exactly rush off to the leisure centre every time she felt tempted by a slice of hot toast slathered in butter. She needed something she could do at eight in the morning, at ten at night, and any time in between, which didn't involve specialist equipment or membership of a gym.

The only thing she could think of was good old-fashioned walking and Picklewick was perfect for that. Surrounded by rolling farmland and not-too high mountains, the village was set in stunning countryside. But once again, she had her doubts: she was under no illusion that after a long and busy day at work she would be extremely reluctant to unwedge her behind from the sofa to go for a brisk walk.

What she needed was a walking buddy. Someone to bully her into going when she didn't feel like it, someone to hold her accountable. Someone who wouldn't take no for an answer and made sure she put her trainers on and went out there.

A lightbulb flashed in her head, and in its wake it left a very distinct image in her mind's eye.

What she needed was *a dog.*

'AW, DAD, THAT'S a crappy thing to happen,' was Cameron's response when Elijah plucked up the courage to tell him that their dream of running the Marathon de Sable together had gone up in smoke.

'Are they sure? I mean, could they have made a mistake?'

Elijah shook his head. 'I asked for a second opinion.'

'Man, that sucks,' his son declared.

Elijah heartily agreed with him.

'But you'll still be able to go running, right?'

'I don't think I will.' Elijah had given it a lot of thought – it was all he'd been able to think about – and he knew he would be risking permanent disability if he went against medical advice.

No more marathons for him. No more running. A gentle jog was the best he could hope for, and even then he'd have to make sure the surface he was on wasn't too hard. Which basically meant a lap or two of the park on the grass. It wouldn't be worth the bother of putting his trainers on for that.

Cameron was looking concerned. 'What will you do? I've never known you not to run. Mum used to say—' He broke off, twin spots of colour appearing in his cheeks.

'It's okay. I know what your mother used to say.' She'd said it to his face enough times, so Elijah didn't need to hear it second hand. His addiction to keeping fit (okay, to *running*) hadn't been the cause of their breakup, but it hadn't helped that he'd used to spend inordinate amounts of time pounding the streets, lanes, and hillsides in his quest to run a route in his best time ever. Elijah didn't so much race against other people when he took part in a marathon, because there would always be someone faster than him (that was a fact of life) – he raced against *himself*. It also hadn't helped that whenever an argument loomed, Elijah used to don his trainers and disappear out the door. He'd been a gold medallist in avoiding confrontation. 'Emotionally absent,' his ex-wife used to say. And maybe she'd had a point. 'Selfish' was something else she'd called him. And maybe she'd had a point there, as well.

It was all water under the bridge now, of course. They'd split over a decade ago, when Cameron was only twelve. It had been hard on the boy, but Elijah had tried his damnedest to be a good father and a good role model – as much as he could, at least. He worked hard, didn't drink to excess, and didn't have any vices apart from an addiction to running marathons. And he'd spent as much time with his son as possible, only moving from Thornbury to Picklewick after Cameron had passed his driving test and had become more mobile. The stars had all aligned at that point, because the bakery had come on the market at roughly the same time and Elijah had leapt at the chance to buy it. Not because he loved what he did (by then he'd become rather indifferent), but because it had given him the opportunity to be his own boss, which in turn allowed him more flexibility when it came to the hours he worked, so he could go for longer runs whenever he wanted. See, he said to himself, his life had revolved around running. What the hell was it going to revolve around now that he'd had the one thing he lived for, taken away from him?

'I don't know what I'm going to do,' he admitted, in answer to Cameron's question. 'Take up golf maybe, or lawn bowls.'

'*You*, take up *golf?*' Cameron scoffed. 'You'd hate it. And I can't see you playing bowls, neither.'

'Why not?' Elijah hadn't been serious about bowls; however, he was curious as to why his son couldn't envisage him playing the game.

'You're too much of a loner.'

'Is that what you think?'

'It's what I know. I'm like you in that respect. I've always hated team sports. Don't mind watching them, but don't want to take part in them.'

'What do you suggest?'

Cameron became sombre as he asked, 'You will be able to walk properly, won't you?'

'I hope so!' Elijah replied. 'I mean, the bone has mended, so there shouldn't be any reason why I won't be able to. I've got a bit of a limp now, but that's only because I had to wear that boot. I've been doing stretches and stuff to strengthen it.'

'Why not take up hiking?'

'What, like stroll around on my own?'

Cameron shook his head. 'No, not *stroll*. A fast walk.'

'Where would I walk to? All my local routes will just remind me that I should be running them.'

'Find some new ones.'

Elijah blew out his cheeks. He knew he was being negative and probably coming across as awkward and obstinate, but – damn it! – he didn't *want* to find new anything. He wanted his life to go back to the way it was before.

'And if you don't want to go for a hike on your own,' Cameron continued, 'get a dog.'

'A *dog?*' Elijah was incredulous. 'I'm at work all day.'

Cameron raised his eyebrows. 'Five-thirty til one-thirty isn't all day.'

'It's a seven-hour day, six days a week. I don't have the time. And when I'm not at work, I'm running.' As soon as the day's baking was complete and the kitchen was scrubbed ready for tomorrow, he was out the door.

'But you won't be running anymore,' Cameron reminded him. 'A dog will get you out of the house and keep you company, too.' He looked incredibly pleased with himself.

'A dog,' Elijah repeated.

'Yeah, something big and active. One that'll like going out for hours. Not a lap dog.'

'And where do you suggest I get this fictional dog from?'

'The Forever Home Kennels, of course!'

'Of course. Why didn't I think of that?' he grumbled.

But the more he thought about it, the better the idea seemed, and he found himself reaching for his phone.

CHAPTER FOUR

MONDAY MORNING saw Nora stepping stark naked on the bathroom scales and glaring at the display in disbelief. Weight loss: half a pound. Was that *all?* Considering she'd had almost three full days of eating leaves, she'd hoped she would have lost more. She also felt dreadful: nausea, tummy ache, headache, weak and lethargic. What she needed was proper food, such as bread, potatoes, rice, pasta, biscuits...

Last week, when she'd been telling Trinny about her diagnosis, she'd had no intention of going cold turkey, but since her eyesight scare on Friday, and after doing some research (lots of research), she realised the best way to reduce her blood glucose to non-diabetic levels was to lose weight *fast*. Which meant not eating *anything* carby – because if she had one biscuit, she'd have to eat the whole packet.

Nora Bunting, she'd said to herself, *you've got no self- control. It's got to be all or nothing.* And in her case, she had to settle for nothing. Which meant that she hadn't gone to the tapas bar as planned on Saturday evening and neither had she gone to The Black Horse for Sunday lunch. Right now, she was feeling woefully deprived and extremely depressed. And seeing the meagre weight loss wasn't doing anything for her mood.

'One day at a time,' she muttered, as she threw on some clothes and contemplated breakfast. But maybe her motto should be 'one meal at a time' she thought after she'd eaten it, because the berries and yoghurt might look healthy and wholesome, but she may as well have eaten fresh air since it failed to fill her up.

Disheartened, she wondered how much longer she'd be able to keep this up. No wonder she'd never bothered dieting in the past; she must have sub-consciously realised how awful it would be. Maybe increasing the exercise instead, would be a more realistic way forward than restricting her food intake?

She was trying to think how best to fit more exercise into her day (okay, fit in *some* exercise, since she didn't actually do *any at all* at the moment) when she arrived at the salon. Her idea of getting a dog was something she was still considering, and she'd spent most of last night mulling it over – when she hadn't been thinking about food, that is. There were pros and cons to dog ownership, and she had to make sure the pros outweighed the cons, and that this was something she really wanted and could seriously commit to. Plus, at least when her mind had been occupied with a puppy, it hadn't been on the chocolate chip cookie and the caramel latte she'd been craving.

Nora decided to canvas opinions. 'I'm thinking about getting a dog,' she announced, while putting layers into Dulcie Fairfax's hair.

Kendra gaped at her. 'A dog? *You?* Why?'

'Is it really so outlandish?' Nora was taken aback.

'A dog needs walking, like daily, and I don't mean to the shops.'

'I know; that's the point. Not the whole point, of course,' she added hurriedly. 'It'll also be good company.'

'You're never in!'

Nora drew herself up to her full height. 'I'll have you know I stayed in all weekend.'

'Were you not feeling well?' Kendra teased, then hesitated. 'Actually, Nora, you do look a bit peaky. Are you okay? I noticed you haven't been to the bakers this morning.'

Lori piped up, 'She didn't go on Friday, either. And she's not touched the chocolate digestives I brought in.'

'And you weren't in on Saturday,' Kendra added.

'I told you; I had to go to the opticians because my reading glasses broke. I'm fine, honestly.' She wasn't fine, and she was also fibbing. But she wasn't ready to tell her staff just yet; she needed to get her own head around it first. All they needed to know was that she wanted to be a bit healthier, and a dog might help her achieve that.

'We were talking about me getting a dog,' she reminded them. 'What do you think, Dulcie, since I can't get any sense out of this lot?' She sidled around to stand in front of her client and checked the length of the hair at the sides, pulling down the strands to make sure they were even.

'It's a commitment and a dog can be a lot of work,' Dulcie said.

'Do you have a dog?'

'No, but my sister runs The Forever Home Boarding Kennels on Muddypuddle Lane, so I get to hear all about it,' Dulcie explained. 'And I get to cuddle a puppy now and again.'

'Puppies are *so* cute,' Lori said dreamily.

'Puppies are even more work than adult dogs,' Dulcie pointed out. 'House training, training in general, then there's the chewing. Would you get a puppy?' she asked Nora.

When the idea of having a dog had first occurred to her, Nora must admit that she'd had a vision of an adorable ball of cute fluffiness, but she was now having second thoughts.

Lori said, 'We've got a dog. For the first few nights after we brought her home, she howled the place down. It only took a couple of weeks to house train her, though.' She laughed. 'My mum said she had to have eyes in the back of her head, because whenever her back was turned

Pippin would do a wee, or worse. And she used to chew *everything*. She ate my watch strap once, and we were on pins until it came out the other end.'

Nora shuddered, not wanting to contemplate what *that* might have involved. 'On second thoughts, maybe a puppy wouldn't be a good idea. I can't have it pooping and peeing in the salon.'

Lori's eyes widened. 'You'd bring it to work?'

'Absolutely. I couldn't leave it at home on its own all day. That wouldn't be fair.' Nora hesitated. She had to make sure her staff were happy with this, and she was also worried that she might be making a mistake. 'Would you be okay with that?' She ruffled her fingers through the back of Dulcie's hair, watching to see how it fell.

'No objections from me,' Kendra said.

'What about you, Lori? I know you're on work placement and you're not a member of staff as such, but your opinion still counts.'

'I don't mind, I love dogs. What sort would you get?'

'A small one,' Nora replied.

'Boy or girl?'

'Girl.'

'Smooth coat or fluffy?'

'Smooth.' Nora laughed. 'I see enough hair at work; I don't want to have to spend hours grooming a fluffy dog when I'm at home.'

'If you do go ahead and get a dog,' Dulcie said, 'please consider a rescue. There are so many adorable dogs looking for someone to love them. The Forever Home helps out the animal sanctuary in

Thornbury by housing some of the dogs they don't have room for, and they have several rescues there now, if you wanted to go see them. They're open between two and four today. I could let Maisie know if you wanted to pop along; she's my sister.'

Nora bit her lip. Was this moving too fast? Should she take more time to think about it? As Dulcie said, owning a dog was a big responsibility. It wasn't a whim or a fashion accessory; it was a lifetime commitment.

Was she prepared for that? Not really, but neither had she been prepared for the news that she had diabetes, and that was a lifetime thing, too.

Nora's lifestyle had to change drastically, and she knew she couldn't do it all by herself. She needed help, and if that help arrived on four paws, she'd take it.

As she held the mirror up for Dulcie to see the back of her hair, Nora made a decision. 'If you can manage without me for an hour, Kendra, I'd love to go visit The Forever Home this afternoon.'

WAS ELIJAH FEELING excited or apprehensive? It was difficult to tell. Both, probably. Getting a dog was a big decision, especially since he'd never owned one before. What if he was a crap owner? What if the dog didn't like him?

The person he'd spoken to on the phone earlier had told him they'd do their best to ensure they found the right dog for him, but what if *he* wasn't the right person for the *dog?* The woman must have sensed his concern because she'd suggested he popped along to The Forever Home on

Muddypuddle Lane to have a chat with a guy called Jakob, who was responsible for the rescue dogs there.

No time like the present, he'd thought, on learning that he could visit it this afternoon, so as soon as the final batch of baked goods was out of the oven and in the display counter in the shop, he was out the door.

The Forever Home Kennels were on the outskirts of Picklewick, up a steep lane lined with hedgerows and flanked on either side by fields in which horses peacefully grazed. The road led past a riding stable, and then a farm, before heading towards the top of the mountain. The kennels was situated on rolling moorland, and surrounded by tussocky grass, bracken, and wild bilberry bushes, with fantastic views over the village and the valley below.

Elijah knew the area well. He'd run across the mountain more times than he could count, following farm tracks and sheep tracks alike, and he'd seen the previously tumbledown and abandoned old farmhouse transformed by Maisie Fairfax and her partner Adam, into a beautiful house. Maisie had then opened a boarding kennel, since it was the perfect out-of-the-way location to care for numerous noisy dogs, but he hadn't realised that the kennels also helped the animal rescue centre in Thornbury by housing those dogs they didn't have room for.

Reluctantly, Elijah had driven up Muddypuddle Lane, unsure whether his newly healed leg would be up to the task of walking up it, and when he scrambled out of the car he could already hear the voices of several dogs, and his heart began to race.

Eager to meet them, he followed a sign that said "Reception" and found himself in a wooden shed-type building with a counter, behind which sat a young woman with long blond hair tied up in a ponytail.

'Hi, I'm Maisie. How can I help?'

'I'm here about a rescue dog? I'm thinking about adopting one.'

 'In that case, you need to see Jakob. He runs the rescue centre side of things. I'll give him a shout for you.'

A few minutes later, a large bear of a man appeared. He didn't smile, but nodded a greeting and got straight down to business, firing a succession of questions at him until Elijah felt like he was being interrogated by the police.

'Sorry, had to ask,' Jakob explained gruffly. 'It's part of the adoption procedure. We need to make sure you're the right fit. These dogs have had enough upheaval in their lives, and our mission is to find them their forever homes. So,' he continued, 'to recap: you've never had a dog before, you've got a secure garden, and although you work, you're home in the afternoons and evenings. You used to run marathons, but you've had to give it up, so you're looking for an active dog that you can take on long walks. Have I got that right?'

'Spot on,' Elijah said.

The man pressed his lips together thoughtfully, then said, 'Okay, I've got a couple of dogs in mind. Would you like to take a look?'

'Yes, please!' Elijah's pulse quickened as he followed Jakob outside and across a yard towards the kennel blocks, and as they approached, the noise grew louder.

'Not all the dogs in the centre are available for re-homing right now,' Jakob explained. 'Some have medical needs which we're in the process of treating, others have behavioural issues that need to be addressed before we can put them up for adoption, and some have yet to be assessed.'

Elijah glanced into each kennel as they walked slowly past, and was relieved to see they were spacious, clean, and had both indoor and outdoor areas, although the outdoor bits were covered over to protect the dogs from the elements. Each one contained a comfy bed, a water bowl, a selection of toys – and a *dog*.

A succession of inquisitive noses and hopeful eyes peered out, and as each little face tugged at his heartstrings, Elijah had a sudden urge to take all of them home with him.

'Okay, here's the first dog I've got in mind that might be perfect for you,' Jakob announced, coming to a halt in front of a pen containing a tall, golden-coloured dog. 'This little lady is called Xanadu, and she's a Greyhound/German Shepherd cross. She's two-years old, intelligent, active, and friendly. She's got a sweet nature, although she can be a little boisterous at times.'

Elijah gazed at her. Xanadu came up to the bars and stuck her nose through, her tail wagging.

'She's lovely,' he said, and was about to ask if he could meet her properly, when the dog in the next pen caught his eye. The animal was *smiling* at him. Its tongue was lolling, and its mouth was turned up at the corners. Elijah had seen dogs panting before, but this wasn't a pant. 'Is that dog smiling?' he asked.

'Biscuit?' Jakob laughed. 'He does that a lot. He's a friendly chap. In fact, he was one of the other dogs I thought might be a good match for you.'

As though understanding that his future happiness might be on the line, Biscuit lay down and rolled onto his back, exposing his fluffy belly, and wagged his tail. His happy expression had become a pleading one.

Elijah's heart melted. 'What breed is he?' he asked. Not that it mattered, because Elijah liked what he saw.

'A Bernese Mountain Dog. He's three years old, nearly four, and loves everyone. There's not a nasty bone in his body. He's a real people-pleaser. But don't let the goofy expression and fluff ball appearance fool you – he's going to need a fair bit of exercise. These dogs were bred as working dogs.'

'That's exactly what he'll get with me, plenty of exercise,' Elijah said, crouching down and holding out his hand.

Biscuit, perhaps sensing that his "please love me" act might be getting him somewhere, leapt to his feet with alacrity and shoved his wet nose into Elijah's palm.

Elijah laughed when Biscuit licked his hand.

Jakob said, 'Do you want me to fetch him out? See how he behaves without a barrier between you?'

'Absolutely!'

'I've got to warn you that Berners can shed heavily, especially in the spring and autumn when they blow their undercoats.

You need to be prepared for that and groom him regularly,' Jakob advised, his hand on the bolt. 'And they don't like being left alone for long. He'll be able to cope with a few hours, as long as he has plenty of mental stimulation and physical exercise. In other words, wear him out and he'll be okay.'

'I think I can manage all that.' Elijah, never one for late nights, would simply get up a little earlier and take the dog for a nice long walk before work, for an hour, maybe. Then another, longer one when he got home. 'Exercise is one thing any dog of mine will get a lot of,' he assured him.

Jakob opened the door, using his body to prevent Biscuit from escaping, and once he'd brought the dog out, he gestured for Elijah to come closer. Biscuit, bless him, sat at Elijah's feet and smiled again.

'He's gorgeous,' he said, kneeling down to ruffle the dog's ears. His fur was soft and dense, and Elijah buried his fingers in it.

Biscuit licked him on the nose.

'I think it's safe to say he likes you,' Jakob laughed.

'And I like him. I really want to take him home with me right now. Don't worry, I know I can't,' he added. 'Where do we go from here?'

'If you're sure Biscuit is a good fit for you, you'll need to fill in an application form. Once that's done, we'll arrange a home visit to see if your house and garden are suitable. I'm sure they will be, but that's the procedure. Biscuit has already had a thorough health check, but we'll give him another before you collect him. And that's all there is to it.'

'It sounds straightforward.'

'It is, as a rule.'

Elijah, his arm around the dog, who'd scooted into his side and was now leaning on him, pressed his lips together. This was a big decision. Not something to be taken lightly. If he adopted Biscuit, he would hopefully be looking after him for the next decade, so he had to be sure he was doing the right thing.

'Can I have a day or two to think about it?'

'You can take as long as you need,' Jakob said. 'I can't guarantee he'll still be here if you leave it a couple of weeks, but there'll be other dogs. There are *always* other dogs.'

Elijah promised he'd be in touch shortly, and as he returned to his car, he knew he had some serious thinking to do and—

'Oops!' He hadn't been paying attention to where he was going, and had barrelled around a corner and bumped straight into a woman heading in the opposite direction, almost sending her flying.

'Sorry, sorry,' he babbled. 'I wasn't looking where I was going. Are you okay?'

The woman brushed at her top as Elijah steadied her, his hand on her arm.

'I'm fine, honestly. I wasn't concentrating on where I was going, either. Too eager to find my perfect dog.' She stopped talking and peered at him. 'Don't I know you?'

'You might; I own the bakery in the village.'

Her face cleared. 'Ah, yes, so you do. I think I must be your best customer.'

He thought she looked familiar, but he didn't spend much time in the shop, so he couldn't be sure. He preferred to be out the back, baking. If she was local, he'd probably seen her around, though. He saw a lot of people, especially when he was out on his runs, although he didn't converse with many.

Apologising again, he left her to her quest for her perfect dog and headed home.

It was only when he got there and wondered what he was going to do with himself for the rest of the day, did he realise he'd already found *his* perfect dog. He didn't want any other: he wanted *Biscuit*. Even the pooch's name was perfect.

Taking it as a sign, Elijah got back in his car. He had a dog to give a loving home to!

CHAPTER FIVE

NORA MIGHT FEEL like skipping into The Forever Home's reception area, but her body had other ideas. She was still feeling like pooh, but apparently it was common to feel this way when you suddenly stopped eating the amount of carbs your body was used to. However, she was heartened by the knowledge that she wouldn't feel like this forever.

'I'm not too late to have a look around, am I?' she asked the woman in reception.

'Not at all. Are you looking to re-home a dog?'

'I am! Would you be Maisie, by any chance?'

'That's me, and I'm guessing you're Nora from the salon? Dulcie says she loves her hair, by the way.'

'Customer feedback is always appreciated,' Nora said. 'Is it possible to see some today? Dogs, I mean – I've already seen several customers.' She chuckled at her own joke, feeling unaccountably nervous. From what Dulcie had told her, there was a vetting procedure, and she was keen to make a good impression.

'Jakob will show you around,' Maisie said, gesturing to a large man perched on a chair in the corner.

He looked up as his name was mentioned. 'You're a potential adopter?'

Nora nodded.

'Word's getting around,' he said to Maisie, then back to her, 'You're the second drop in we've had today. Take a seat.'

Nora sat obediently.

'Have you owned a dog before?' he asked.

'When I was a child. Obviously, my parents looked after it, so I've no experience of caring for a dog on my own. But I'm willing to learn,' she added.

'That's good. Why do you want one now? I'm not being nosey,' he said. 'I'm merely trying to ensure that we re-home the right dog with you.'

'Don't I get to choose?' Nora had assumed she'd be able to pick the one she wanted.

'Yes and no,' the man replied cryptically. 'I'll see which dogs might be the best fit for you – and you for them – and we'll take it from there. Why now?' he repeated.

She was trying to think what might be an acceptable reason, but found herself blurting, 'I've got diabetes.'

'Okay...'

She could see Jakob trying to make the connection and failing, so she went on to explain, 'I need to lose weight and increase my exercise.' Which translated, meant that she actually had to start doing *some.*

Jakob didn't look enthralled. 'You've heard the saying that "a dog is for life, not just for Christmas"? You don't have a dog just so you can lose a couple of pounds.'

Nora took a deep breath. 'You don't understand. I've got *this* for life. Diabetes doesn't simply go away when you lose weight. I'm going to have to keep active and watch what I eat forever, because if I don't...' She trailed off and swallowed.

The hard lines of Jakob's face softened. 'I see. I didn't realise.'

'Everyone has heard of diabetes, but most people don't understand what having it actually entails.' She blew out her cheeks. 'If I'm honest, I don't fully understand, either. I'm still trying to get my head around it, and I think it's going to take a while. Getting a dog will be part of my new life, because it's going to need a drastic change.'

Jakob was nodding thoughtfully. 'Okay, so we've established what a dog can do for you; now, what can *you* do for a *dog?*'

'Oh, right. Um, I can give it a loving home, I'll walk it twice a day, it'll come to work with me—'

'What do you do?' Jakob interrupted.

'I'm a hairdresser. I have my own salon in Picklewick.'

'So you're the boss? You don't need to ask permission or wait for a "bring your dog to work "day?'

'I did check with my staff first, to make sure they'd be happy with a dog around the place all the time, and they are,' she added defensively. She'd even phoned Paige, the part-timer who covered Andrea's days off and holidays, and she hadn't minded either. In fact, they all seemed delighted at the prospect.

'Do I take it you're looking for a confident dog who likes people?'

'Does that mean I've passed the test?'

The man smiled. 'It means that you sound like a suitable person to adopt a dog. Just a couple more questions, okay?'

She nodded, wondering what could he possibly ask her now: did he want to know her shoe size, her favourite colour, what she liked to watch on TV, perhaps?

'Are there any children or other pets we need to consider?'

'No.'

'Anyone else in the house, like a partner or an elderly parent?'

'No.'

'What kind of property do you live in?'

'A house.'

'Will the dog have access to a garden, and if so, is it secure?'

'Yes, to both.'

'Last question, I promise; do you need to obtain a landlord's permission to have a dog on the property?'

'No, it's mine, I own it.'

'Great. All done.' Jakob sat back, and Nora let out a sigh.

 She'd never been arrested, but she could now easily imagine what being grilled by the police would feel like, thanks to Jakob and his twenty questions.

'Oh, I forgot to ask,' he began, and when she rolled her eyes, he grinned. 'What sort of dog are you thinking of. Large? Small? Smooth haired? Fluffy? Male or female? And would you consider re-homing a puppy?'

She didn't mind *those* questions. They were fun. 'Definitely not a puppy, because I can't have it doing wees and poops in the salon while I'm cutting someone's hair. Not if I want to keep my customers.'

'Okay, house trained,' he murmured to himself.

'But not too old,' she continued, 'because, you know, I'll get too upset when—' She broke off. 'A girl, I think, and smooth haired. I do enough styling and primping in the salon.'

'So,' he began, counting off points on his fingers. 'Friendly, confident, active, likes cuddles?' He glanced at her for confirmation and she nodded. 'A female, not too old but not a puppy, and smooth-coated. Have I missed anything?'

'I don't think so. Do you have a dog like that?'

'We do. Her name is Shona, and she's a Whippet.'

'Don't Whippets need loads of exercise?' Nora asked worriedly. 'I mean, I'll be taking her out twice a day, but in between she'll need to settle and behave herself.'

'Don't let her looks fool you. Yes, she's quick, but Whippets also love lounging around on the sofa. Would you like to meet her?'

Nora gave a little clap. 'I'd love to.' She could imagine it already, the dog lying on a pink bed, calmly accepting strokes and scritches from her clients. Shona sounded perfect.

'Follow me,' Jakob instructed, and Nora jumped to her feet.

As he led her along a row of kennels, she tried not to look inside; she didn't want to see their poor little faces begging her to take them home and love them, and she tried to close her ears to the barks and whines. But it only took one look, just one sideways glance out of the corner of her eye, and she was immediately smitten.

'Wait,' she said, coming to a halt. 'Is this one available?'

Jakob stopped and turned to look at the dog she was pointing at. 'Yes, but—'

'What's her name?'

'Biscuit, and she's a he. Not only is he the wrong gender, he's large and fluffy. Not what you were looking for.'

The dog was staring at her with big brown eyes, his expression solemn. Then he slowly lay down and rolled over, showing her his tummy.

'Aw!' she cried.

'He keeps doing that.'

'He's adorable.'

'And he knows it.' Jakob was shaking his head, but his eyes were kind.

'Hello, Biscuit,' she crooned, and the dog lumbered to his feet. So much for wanting a smooth, short-haired, smaller animal. This dog came up to the top of her thigh and his mostly black coat was long, with feathers down his legs, and a plume of a tail. But he was so handsome, with his white chest, the white markings on his face, and tan legs, and he had such a loving expression. A bit goofy, too.

When he licked her hand, Nora's insides turned to mush. 'He likes me!' she exclaimed.

'He likes everyone.'

'That's a good thing, isn't it? He'll fit right into the salon.'

'He won't be too big?'

Nora guessed that Jakob was playing Devil's Advocate because Biscuit was the exact opposite to what she'd thought she wanted. But she'd fallen in love, and with a name like Biscuit who could blame her? She'd given up one kind of biscuit, but would gain another. A Biscuit for a biscuit.

'I really want this one,' she said. 'He's perfect. What do I have to do?'

'Don't you want to think about it for a day or so? You could go home, and if you're still certain you want him after a couple of days, you can pop back and fill in an application form or do it online.'

Nora took her phone out of her bag. 'I don't need to think about it.'

'Let's go to the office then, and you can fill the form out there.'

'It's okay, I'll do it now online,' Nora said, brandishing her mobile. 'It won't take long.' She'd already found it on the website as he'd been speaking, and she was now typing away, her thumbs flying over the screen.

'What breed is Biscuit?' she asked, coming to a section asking which breeds she might consider adopting.

'A Bernese Mountain Dog. The breed originated in Switzerland to herd livestock.'

'And now he's going to live in Picklewick and herd me. Okay, all done. Now what?' She was impatient to take the dog home and get him settled in, but she assumed that wasn't going to happen today.

'I'll arrange a home visit and—'

'Can we do that now? Arrange the visit? I'll fit in around you. And you can visit the salon as well, if you want.'

'Are you suggesting I need a haircut?' His tone was deadpan, and it took her a moment to realise he was joking.

'If the cap fits,' she responded in kind. 'Aw, I don't want to leave him. He looks so sad.'

Biscuit had his head lowered and was gazing up at her from under his brows. His eyes seemed almost human.

Jakob said, 'He'll be fine. Assuming we can get all the checks done in a timely manner and there are no hold-ups, you'll be able to take him home in a couple of weeks.'

Nora was dismayed. 'That long?'

'Dawn, who manages the main centre in Thornbury, will review your application and do the home visit, but she's on holiday for two weeks.'

'Can't *you* do it?'

He shook his head. 'Sorry, I can't. But you could come and visit Biscuit a couple of times to let him get used to you. Actually, we encourage that, otherwise it's a big shock for them to suddenly be in a strange place with someone they don't know.'

It was better than nothing, she thought. 'Can I come any time?'

'The Forever Home is open for drop ins every day between two and four p.m. If I'm not here, Maisie or one of the others will sort you out. If you come with me to reception now, I can make sure you've filled the form out properly, and let Maisie know what's going on.'

As they retraced their steps, Nora realised she hadn't asked a pertinent question. 'How did Biscuit come to be here?' She hoped his story wasn't a terrible one.

'Divorce,' Jakob said. 'Neither party was in a position to keep him on. He's clearly been well-loved and well-treated, with no behavioural issues. As far as his personality is concerned, he's an ideal dog for you and I would have suggested you meet him if it wasn't for the fact that physically he's the opposite of what you said you wanted.'

Nora chuckled. He was, wasn't he? But her heart had spoken and she wasn't going to ignore it.

Jakob opened the door to the reception area, gesturing for her to go ahead of him, and when she stepped inside she was surprised to see the baker from earlier. He was standing at the desk, resting his hands on it, his attention on Maisie.

Nora gave him a cursory glance, her mind still on Biscuit, but her eyes travelled back to him almost immediately. Although she hadn't actually spoken to him until today, she'd seen him pounding the streets. Rumour was that he ran marathons in his spare time.

When he turned to see who'd entered, he nodded at her in acknowledgment and she nodded back.

Maisie said, 'Jakob, just the man I wanted. Elijah has filled out an application form, but I was telling him that he'd have to be vetted by Dawn before we can take it any further. Am I right in thinking she's on leave for the next two weeks?'

Jakob pulled a face. 'Um, yes, she is, but…' He took a breath, blew out his cheeks, then turned to the man and said with a sigh, 'You've just applied to adopt Biscuit, haven't you?'

When Nora heard that, her heart dropped like a stone down a well, to land with a plop of dismay in the dark depths of her disappointment.

CHAPTER SIX

NORA BUNTING WASN'T a woman to take anything lying down, and when she wanted something, or had set her mind on something, she went for it. Which was why she owned her own salon. She'd had a vision, and she'd worked hard to make it a reality. But that was her career and her business, and hairdressing was a passion she'd held ever since she'd unwrapped a box containing a disembodied plastic head sporting a mass of fake golden hair one Christmas morning when she was six years old. She'd wanted to play with hair ever since, and she'd been fortunate enough to be able to make a career out of it.

However, this was different. This involved her health, and she was convinced that a dog was just what she needed to help her lose weight and regain control of her glucose levels. It also involved her emotions, because she didn't want *any* dog. She wanted *Biscuit*. Even in that short amount of time, they'd had a connection. She could feel it in her heart. He'd looked deep into her eyes, and she'd seen the adoration in them. He wanted *her* to be his new owner. He'd been silently begging her to take him home, and she wasn't going to let him down.

When she heard Jakob say to the baker, 'You've applied to adopt Biscuit,' her heart had sunk. But she soon rallied, and before the man could open his mouth, she snapped, 'You can't have him! He's mine.'

'Um, technically, he doesn't belong to either of you,' Jakob pointed out. 'By filling in an application form, you've expressed an interest, nothing more.'

'Well, *I'm* more interested than *he* is,' Nora shot back.

'I saw him first,' Elijah retorted. Then had second thoughts, and said, 'Didn't I?' He turned to Jakob. 'You didn't tell me someone else was interested?' His tone was accusing.

'That's because no one was,' Jakob replied calmly.

'Then I *did* see him first!' Elijah cried.

Nora scowled. 'I'm sure Jakob would have told me if someone had already applied to adopt him.' She turned a glare on Jakob.

He held up his hands. 'I didn't realise Elijah had. He was going home to think about it.'

Nora rounded on the baker. 'Ha! So when you almost knocked me over just now, you were on your way home. Ergo—' she paused, dredging the word out of hours of watching crime and courtroom dramas on TV, '—*I* applied for him first.'

Elijah's mouth dropped open. 'You can't have! I've just filled the form in, five minutes ago.'

'I did it online – *ten* minutes ago.' She turned to Jakob. 'It *was* about ten minutes, wasn't it?'

Jakob, who was already a tall man, seemed to Nora to grow in stature. 'Calm down, people,' he said, raising his voice. 'It doesn't matter who saw the dog first, or whose application form was received the soonest. The only thing I'm interested in is what's best for Biscuit. Who will give him the home he needs, and the home he deserves, and it mightn't be either of you.'

'*What?*' Nora cried, astounded.

Elijah was shaking his head. 'Why wouldn't it be me? *I* can give him all the exercise he needs.' He looked at her out of the corner of his eye.

Nora bristled. If that was a sly dig at her weight, she wasn't going to be responsible for her actions.

'I run marathons—' He stopped, flushed pink, then amended, 'I *used to* run marathons, but even if I won't be running them anymore, I'll walk him for miles.'

'Funny that,' Nora said archly. 'I can put one foot in front of the other, too. You don't have a monopoly on walking.'

She was relieved to hear that he was no longer running marathons, because she couldn't compete with that. The last time she'd done anything remotely like running, was when she'd made a dash to the bar the other week because they'd called last orders and she'd wanted to get a final drink in before the landlord kicked her, Trinny, and the rest of the customers out.

She intercepted another look, this time a head-to-toe scan that lingered fleetingly on her waist, then her face, before darting away. Nora glowered in response.

Elijah said, 'He won't be left on his own for long if he comes to live with me.' To Nora's ears, he was starting to sound desperate as he added, 'I'm usually home from work by one thirty in the afternoon.'

'Hah!' Nora crowed. She could trump *that*. 'He won't be left on his own at all if *I* adopt him, because I'm going to take him into work with me!'

Elijah visibly deflated. There wasn't much of him to begin with, but now he seemed to shrink in on himself.

Taking pity on him, her voice grew softer as she said, 'There are loads of other dogs to choose from. It doesn't have to be Biscuit.'

His expression darkened. 'Back at ya, darlin'! Why don't you get yourself a cute little poodle; something a bit more manageable?'

'What makes you think I won't be able to manage Biscuit? Jakob thinks I can. He's all for me adopting him.'

'Whoa, I didn't say that,' Jakob protested, and Nora blushed as she realised she'd gone too far.

But once again, she rallied. 'Depending on Dawn at the Thornbury Centre giving me the go ahead,' she amended, adding, 'I can't see any reason why she won't.'

'I can't see any reason why she won't support *my* application, either,' Elijah countered.

Jakob intervened. 'Okay, folks, there's nothing further that can be done at the moment, so I suggest you go home and wait for Dawn to contact you. And if you're not successful in adopting Biscuit, I hope you'll consider one of the other dogs who desperately need a loving home.'

Nora wanted to stay and argue her case, but she knew it was pointless. The decision of who would adopt Biscuit wasn't Jakob's to make. She knew she was in a strong position – her house and garden were perfect for a dog, he wasn't going to be left on his own while she was in work, and although she didn't look particularly athletic, she thought she'd be able to convince the centre manager that she was committed to walking Biscuit every day.

But might there be any way to make her case even stronger? As Nora returned to her car, it occurred to her that maybe there *was* something she could do.

She hadn't imagined the connection between her and the dog, so what if she worked on that? She could demonstrate her commitment to the pooch by showing up every day and spending some time with him.

She didn't know whether Biscuit's preference would be taken into consideration, but she was going to make damn sure that if he was asked, *she* would be the dog's first choice.

ELIJAH WATCHED Nora Bunting stalk out the door, her nose in the air, her hips swaying, and he scowled at her confidence. He knew in his heart that he would be a better owner for Biscuit, Nora taking the dog to work with her notwithstanding.

He lamented, 'I thought Biscuit had taken to me.'

'I hope this hasn't put you off adopting,' Jakob said. 'Would you like another look at Xanadu, or I could show you the other dog I have in mind?'

'Go on, then,' he replied, not really wanting to meet any other dogs, but maybe it would be a good idea in case he was turned down for Biscuit.

Although, if he *was* turned down for Biscuit, didn't it follow that he'd probably be turned down for the others as well?

The thought made him flinch. Was there any point in carrying on, he wondered, but when he neared Biscuit's kennel and saw that expectant face and those loving eyes once more, Elijah knew he couldn't give up on him; not while there was hope. Until he was officially told that he wouldn't be Biscuit's new owner, he would continue to fight.

Although, exactly how he was going to do that was something he'd yet to work out. Would bribery work? Could he say to Dawn, *if you let me adopt Biscuit, you can have all the pastries, bread, and cake you want?* Or would Nora bribe her with free haircuts for the rest of her life?

He had a feeling Nora wasn't going to give up, either. She was rather lovely – dark-haired, amber-eyed, a face made for laughter, a curvy figure – but she was also stubborn, opinionated, confrontational and selfish, so no matter how attractive she might be on the outside, on the inside she was as irritating as hell. And he didn't just think that because she seemed determined to win Biscuit at all costs.

Not that the dog was a prize to be won. If Elijah didn't genuinely believe *he* was the best person to adopt him, he would have retreated gracefully.

Jakob broke into his thoughts. 'Why do I get the feeling this kennel is as far as we're going to get?'

'Because it's true?'

'I thought as much.' The man sighed. 'Believe me, I get it. Some dogs just touch you here.' He placed a meaty hand on his chest.

Biscuit whined for attention, which Elijah happily gave him, ruffling his ears through the bars of the pen. Elijah recalled how happy he'd been driving back up Muddypuddle Lane, how he'd been planning their lives together, his and Biscuit's: where the dog would sleep, where they'd go walking, what toys he'd buy him. And now... *Now* he was going to have to say goodbye to him, possibly for good.

'Sorry, boy, I've got to go,' he said to Biscuit, whose eyes were closed in bliss at having his ears fondled.

Elijah looked up at Jakob; there was something playing on his mind, something he'd read on the sanctuary's website...

Ah ha! He got it!

'It says on your website that dogs can meet their potential owners several times to give them a chance to build a bond. Will it help if I build a bond with Biscuit? I mean, I can't see any reason why Dawn would think I'm *not* suitable to re-home him.'

Jakob sighed. 'You can visit him as many times as you like. The centre is open between two and four every afternoon.'

Elijah pulled a face. 'Is that a good idea? I'm worried he might become too attached to me, and be disappointed if I'm not able to have him.'

Jakob sighed again. 'Biscuit is a bright boy, but I don't think he understands that you want to adopt him. Yes, he'll form a bond with you, but it won't be any different to the bond he has with me, or Maisie, or any of the other staff who care for him. It's you I'm concerned about. I don't want *you* getting too attached to *him*.'

'I'll be fine,' Elijah said. 'No need to worry about me.'

And the reason Jakob needn't worry was that Elijah was going to do everything in his power to prove that *he* was the best dog parent for this particular dog.

CHECKING THE RUNMAD app several times a day was something Elijah did out of habit, and because he was interested to see what the other Madders were up to. It wasn't just races that were posted: the vast majority of posts were training runs since not everyone entered races, and some people only ever did fun runs or park runs. Elijah was just as interested in long distance runs for pure enjoyment as he was in competitions. What he liked to see were times, distances, and elevation. And route maps, because the app allowed people to post those, too.

Sitting on the sofa with a cup of tea, Elijah scrolled through today's posts, giving people "kudos" and writing encouraging comments.

On telling one of the guys who he followed regularly that he'd done a great job in running twenty-six miles this morning (it was actually yesterday for the guy, because he lived in New Zealand – RunMad was a global app), Elijah received an instant reply wanting to know when he was going to post his next run.

Elijah placed the phone on the cushion next to him and dropped his head back. It was common to post details of injuries, usually accompanied by photos of braces or the athletic tape used to strap up and support joints and muscles, and he'd been no exception. After he'd uploaded a photo of his boot, he'd had a slew of comments offering sympathy, commiseration and encouragement. It was all part of the supportive RunMad community.

However, he suddenly realised he wasn't part of that community anymore. He had posted his final run although he hadn't known it at the time, and sadness swept over him, accompanied by a feeling of loss. It was doing him no good seeing the runs that others posted, seeing the camaraderie, the banter, the praise...

It was probably for the best if he deleted the app off his phone. He wouldn't be missed by more than a handful of people, and even they would forget him after a while. If they hadn't already.

However, old habits died hard, and he found himself reaching for his phone once again and searching for his son's profile.

Cameron had posted a fifteen-mile run this morning captioned "short stretch of the legs", and Elijah felt a surge of pride. The emotion was bittersweet, since it was also accompanied by sorrow that he would never again be able to go out for a run with his son. There was no point in thinking that maybe a short run wouldn't hurt, because he didn't do short runs. To him, three miles wasn't worth getting out of bed for. And Cameron wouldn't appreciate it, either. Besides, Elijah was fully aware that if he broke into a jog, he'd end up doing thirteen miles until he was back to putting in the same mileage as before – and he'd keep going until he injured himself once more. The consultant had been very clear about what would happen if he did.

Quietly, without fanfare, Elijah deleted the app.

And felt as though he'd deleted part of himself.

WHEN NORA POPPED into the salon for the last hour or so before closing that afternoon, everything appeared to be under control.

'Thanks for helping out, Paige,' she said to the part-time stylist, who usually only covered Kendra's day off and during really busy times like prom season or Christmas.

'I'm happy to,' Paige replied. 'In fact, I'm looking for a few more hours, if there are any going. I want to take the kids to Disneyland at Christmas, so I'd better start saving now.'

'Ooh, nice! They'll love it!' Kendra exclaimed. 'I took mine a few years back, and when Daryl and I went to Paris for a long weekend, we went to Disneyland on our own.'

'Yeah, I'm looking forward to it,' Paige said, 'but it isn't going to be cheap.'

Nora was almost clapping her hands with glee: she'd been wondering how to wrangle a full appointment book with disappearing off to Muddypuddle Lane every afternoon for the next two weeks, and Paige was offering her the ideal solution.

'So you found a dog you want but you don't know whether you can have it, because the guy who owns the bakery wants it as well?' Kendra summarised after Nora explained what had happened that afternoon. 'How will they decide?'

'I'm not totally sure, but I want to give it my best shot, so I'm going to spend as much time with Biscuit as I can, so if you—'she turned to Paige '—can do every afternoon for the next couple of weeks that'll be a big help.'

'Count me in.' Paige beamed.

'Does it have to be that particular dog?' Kendra asked. 'I mean, he's not the only one there, is he? And won't a big dog like that need a lot of exercise? I know you said you wanted to lose a couple of pounds, but I can't see you traipsing around the streets on a cold winter evening after a day at work. Have you really thought this through? Why don't you try a slimming club? At least you can stop going to a club if you get fed up.'

Kendra wore a perplexed expression, and Nora realised it was time she confided in her. The woman had worked with her for twelve years, so was more of a friend than an employee, but Nora didn't want the others to know so she said, 'Paige and Lori, you can get off. Kendra and I will finish up here.' The last client of the day was done and dusted, and there was only a bit of tidying up left to do.

Nora felt Kendra's eyes on her and knew she'd guessed something was up, but Kendra waited until the others had left before she said anything.

'What's going on, Nora?'

Nora steeled herself and said, 'I've got diabetes.'

Kendra blew out a breath, ruffling her bangs. 'I knew something was wrong. You've been acting all weird, and I didn't think it was the menopause, either. Aw, hon, it'll be alright. Shall I pop the kettle on? We can have a cuppa while you tell me all about it, and I think there's those packet of chocolate digestives in the cupboard, to go with.'

'I can't, I've got diabetes,' Nora repeated.

'Surely one won't hurt? It's not like you're going to eat the whole packet, or they've even got that much sugar in them.'

But that was the problem. One *would* hurt because she wouldn't be able to stop at one. Her biscuit eating days were over: Nora had an entirely different kind of Biscuit on her mind now.

CHAPTER SEVEN

DESPITE NORA BEING twenty minutes early (the animal sanctuary didn't officially open its doors until two p.m.), Elijah was there ahead of her, lounging against the wall of the reception area, arms folded, legs crossed. He was wearing jeans, trainers and a tee shirt, and she suspected he'd walked up Muddypuddle Lane this afternoon. To prove a point, obviously.

Nora vowed to do the very same thing tomorrow. She needed to show that she was just as— What? *Fit?* Hardly. Able to walk that distance comfortably? That would be a better description. It was also a goal, because at the moment she wasn't entirely sure she *could* walk from the centre of Picklewick to The Forever Home Kennels since quite a bit of it was uphill!

But wasn't that the reason she was here, to get fit? It was barely a week since she'd been given her diagnosis, and this morning when she'd stood on the scales she'd seen a reduction (yippee!) but she still felt like rubbish (boo!). However, the rubbish feeling should pass any day now, as soon as her body became accustomed to having less sugar circulating in her bloodstream.

Yeah, well, her *body* might get used to it, but her taste buds hadn't: every time she saw cake, chocolate, crisps, bread (the list of things she couldn't have was endless), her mouth watered and she was hit by an intense craving that she had to battle hard to resist. So far she'd managed it, but it hadn't been easy, and she had a feeling it wasn't going to get any better. Being here was taking her mind off her cravings though, because how could she think about sweet food when she had a sweet pup to concentrate on and a not-so-sweet baker to oust?

Jakob took one look at the pair of them and sighed loudly. The poor man seemed to be sighing an awful lot, and she suspected she and Elijah were to blame.

'I hope you're not going to give me grief?' he warned, looking from one to the other.

Nora shook her head vigorously as Elijah said, 'I just want to give Biscuit the opportunity to get used to me.'

'So do I,' Nora stated, in case Jakob had forgotten why she was there.

Jakob didn't look convinced. 'Should I give you time slots?'

Actually, Nora *would* prefer to see Biscuit on her own, but she also wanted to see how Biscuit interacted with Elijah, so she quickly leapt in with, 'I'm sure that won't be necessary. We're both adults, after all.' She caught a flash of a scowl on her rival's face and suppressed a smirk.

'I was hoping I could take him for a walk,' Elijah said. 'A big dog like him needs a lot of exercise.' His sideways glance at her was pointed.

'That's just what I was going to say,' Nora fibbed.

'We could take him together?' Elijah suggested, and Nora narrowed her eyes. He was up to something, but she wasn't sure what.

'Maybe next time,' Jakob said. 'You can take him to the exercise field instead. It's secure, so you can let him off. He likes playing fetch.'

When Elijah's face fell, Nora guessed he'd been hoping to out-walk her, to go so fast that she'd soon be out-paced and left behind, and she shot Jakob a grateful smile. When Jakob didn't respond, she realised he hadn't vetoed the walk for *her* benefit. He'd done it because he didn't trust them.

Oh, dear, that didn't bode well for her or for Elijah, if Jakob didn't think either of them was capable of looking after the dog they were hoping to adopt.

'Good idea,' she said. 'It'll let him get used to me first, before I take him out.'

'Get *you* used to how strong *he* is,' Elijah countered. 'I reckon you'll struggle to hold him.'

Nora gave him a scathing look. 'I've probably got a better chance of holding him than you.' She flexed her arm, showing off a muscle that she didn't actually have or if she did, it was hidden by a pudgy covering of flesh. Still, she was confident *she'd* be able to control the dog, and Mr Weedy *wouldn't*. He didn't look as though he'd be able to hold a Chihuahua back.

'Actually, Biscuit walks nicely on the lead,' Jakob told them. 'He's very well-mannered.'

Nora had a feeling he thought *they* weren't, but was too polite to say.

'I'll bring him over to the exercise field for you,' he told them, his tone brooking no argument.

Nora replied brightly, 'Great, we'll see you there.' She was determined to prove that she, for one, could play nice. If Elijah couldn't, that was his lookout and it wouldn't do him any favours in the long run.

After Jakob pointed out where they needed to go, Nora didn't wait for Elijah but headed off at a rate of knots.

After a brief pause, he caught up and fell into step. 'Dogs can sense emotions, you know,' he said.

'Is that your thought for the day?'

'Just saying.'

'No need. I was already aware of that pearl of wisdom. I've had dogs in the past.'

He looked crestfallen. 'You're an experienced dog owner, then?'

'Experienced-ish.' She wanted to lie, but feared Jakob might let the cat out of the bag.

'What do you mean, *ish?*''

 'I had a dog when I was a child.'

'*Ah...*' Elijah nodded sagely, and she had a brief surge of one-upmanship until he followed it with, 'So *your parents* looked after it. I *see.*'

'I helped.'

'How old were you?'

'Six or seven,' she muttered, summoning a brief burst of speed when the entrance to the exercise field came into view.

'As I said,' Elijah crowed, easily keeping up with her, 'your parents looked after it.'

She opened the gate. 'I suppose you've owned dogs before.' Would that be a black mark against her? It would, wouldn't it? Drat! She caught the shifty look on his face as he turned away to close the gate behind him. 'How many dogs have you had? One? *None?*'

'This will be my first,' he admitted.

Result! Not that she was keeping score, but this was one-nil to her. As for everything else, they were roughly level pegging. She topped him on the "dog won't be left on its own much" stakes, and he topped her on the exercise front. But exercise was something she could improve on, whereas he was *never* going to be able to take Biscuit with him to the bakery.

Feeling quietly confident, Nora checked out the field while she awaited the dog's arrival. A high fence surrounded a large grassy area, with a couple of benches dotted around it, and in one corner was a short plastic tunnel and a couple of low jumps. A wooden crate containing a variety of balls and other throwy type toys sat next to the gate, and there was also a standpipe and a water bowl.

When Nora saw Jakob walking towards the field with Biscuit plodding by his side, she could hardly contain her excitement.

'Biscuit!' she called, before they were even inside.

Elijah crouched down and held out his hand. 'Hello, boy; remember me?'

Jakob gave first her, then Elijah, a keen look. 'He's not a toy. If he doesn't want to come to you, don't force the issue.'

'I won't.' Elijah's reply was confident, as Nora said, 'Of course not. We'll let him decide.'

Jakob unclipped the lead from Biscuit's harness.

Biscuit didn't move.

Jakob said, 'I'll be in the kennel block if you need me.' His expression clearly said that he hoped they wouldn't.

'We'll be fine,' Nora assured him with more confidence than she felt. She wished she'd agreed to Jacob's offer of giving them time slots now.

Neither she nor her arch-rival said anything further until Jakob left, then both called the dog simultaneously.

'Hi, Biscuit. Come here, Biscuit,' Nora called, in a high pitched, encouraging tone.

Elijah, the sneaky git, went for a different approach. 'What have I got for you? Come see.' He was holding out his hand, and in the middle of his palm lay a treat.

Elijah was *bribing* him!

Nora wished she'd thought of that. Note to self: bring a variety of treats tomorrow. And a toy.

Obviously Biscuit was tempted by the morsel of food, and triumph flashed across Elijah's face.

Remembering what Jakob had said, Nora armed herself with a ball. 'Fetch!' she yelled, flinging the ball a decent distance, surprising herself. She hadn't thrown a ball of any description since those hateful netball matches at school.

The dog immediately bounded after it in a blur of tail, paws, and fur. He was quick to bring it back and drop it at her feet, and it was Nora's turn to look triumphant. However, her expression quickly became a grimace when she picked up the soggy ball. Ew.

Get over it, she told herself. *It's only a bit of slobber.*

She threw it again and Biscuit chased after it once more, Elijah and his sneaky treats forgotten.

Nora watched the guy out of the corner of her eye, noting the dismayed drop of his shoulders, and for a moment she felt guilty. But all's fair in love and war, and they were warring over the love of this gorgeous dog, so to her mind whatever advantage she could gain was worth it. And she was fairly certain that *he* hadn't felt guilty when he'd stuffed his pockets with doggy treats.

Nora and Biscuit were getting into a rhythm, her throwing, him fetching. It couldn't go on indefinitely though, for two reasons: Nora's arm was beginning to tire (who knew that chucking a ball could be such hard work?), and Biscuit was taking longer and longer to drop the ball, until he eventually sank down onto the grass, his tongue lolling, the ball nestled between his front paws.

'I think I've worn him out,' she declared smugly.

'I think he needs a drink,' Elijah countered, taking the wind out of her sails.

Darn it, he was probably right, but before she could make a move, he'd picked up the chunky metal bowl and was filling it with water from the standpipe. Biscuit got up and trotted over to him, lapping noisily.

Nora retrieved the ball, fully expecting the dog to resume his game once he'd slaked his thirst, but instead Biscuit's attention was caught by the scent of something edible in Elijah's pocket, and she gritted her teeth.

Biscuit sat and offered Elijah his paw.

'Aw, he's saying please,' Elijah said, a smile spreading across his face, and something about his delight tugged at her. It was the first time she'd seen a genuine smile, and it lit him up.

Nora paused to look at him. *Really* look at him, and she liked what she saw. Elijah Grant was tall and thin, wiry rather than skinny, possibly in his early fifties (it was difficult to tell), with grey hair, and the bluest of blue eyes. When he wasn't being a pratt, he seemed quite nice. Not bad looking, either. A slim silver fox, she mused, and a feeling she hadn't experienced in a long time swept through her: attraction.

It kind of put her on the back foot, being so unexpected.

Dismissing the feeling, she brought her focus sharply back to what she could do to counteract his upper hand, because right now, at this precise moment, Biscuit preferred Elijah. But only because the man was feeding him.

Let's see what happens when the treats run out, she told herself. And very soon, they did, because Elijah, in his eagerness to impress Biscuit and keep the dog close, fed him the little morsels one after the other until the dog had scoffed the lot.

Nora, who was observing intently, saw the exact moment when Elijah lost the dog's attention, and she leapt on it.

'Biscuit!' she called, waving the luminous green ball at him. 'Come here, boy.'

Biscuit happily obliged. His tail was waving from side to side like a feather duster, his eyes were bright, and he seemed to be smiling. This dog was having the time of his life. And no wonder, with two attentive humans, endless ball playing, and handfuls of treats.

Nora shot Elijah a smug smile.

Elijah scowled. But the scowl didn't last long, because her arm soon began to ache again, and before long, Nora's throws had once more lost whatever power they'd originally had.

Gleefully, her rival selected a ball of his own and threw it.

Biscuit didn't hesitate. He ran after it, grabbed it, and brought it back to drop at Elijah's feet.

It was Nora's turn to scowl. Inwardly seething and having run out of options, she sat on the nearest bench and sulked. And that was how Jakob found them when he returned a short time later.

'I'm going to have to kick you out,' he said. 'I need the field for a family who want to get to know their potential new pup.'

Elijah groaned in disappointment, but Nora was secretly relieved. This visit had swiftly become a spectator sport and although she loved watching Biscuit, she hadn't wanted to watch him having fun with *Elijah.*

Jacob attached the lead to Biscuit's harness. 'It looks like he's had a good time.'

'Oh, he has!' Elijah enthused. 'He's played a game of fetch, and has had some little treats, and I gave him some water, too.'

Nora's scowl became a full-blown annoyed simmer. From the way Elijah was talking, Jakob must think she'd sat on her backside for the whole time and ignored the dog.

Well, the gloves would be off tomorrow, just see if they wouldn't!

CHAPTER EIGHT

NORA WAS GETTING sick and tired of omelettes for breakfast. She knew eggs were supposed to help regulate her blood glucose, but they didn't hit the spot in the same way that a sticky, flaky Danish pastry did. And not having a caramel latte in the morning was killing her.

Whoever had come up with the theory that eating protein for breakfast would keep you full for the rest of the day, needed to have their head examined because they were wrong, Nora grumbled to herself as she stomped around the village before work.

She was trying to establish a routine prior to bringing Biscuit home, so with that in mind, she'd set her alarm for an hour earlier than usual, had made herself a cheesy omelette, prepared a packed lunch, and was now out for a brisk thirty-minute walk.

It was a glorious morning, but Nora didn't feel glorious. She felt angry: angry at the doctor who'd diagnosed her, angry at the unfairness of it (why *her?*), angry that there was so much yummy, delicious food that she could no longer eat, angry at everything and everyone. *Especially* Elijah Grant, because it was *his* bakery she was marching past and smelling the mouthwatering aroma of freshly baked bread and croissants.

This was what she meant by life not being fair. He was a sodding baker, yet he was as thin as a twig! Didn't he eat any of the stuff he made? He wasn't a good advertisement for his business, was he? What was the old saying about never trusting a skinny cook?

The fact that he was a baker and so slim was bad enough, but why did it have to be *him* who was making a play for Biscuit? Talk about adding insult to injury!

Holding her breath until she was well beyond the enticing smells, she let it out in a whoosh, earning herself a wary look from a delivery driver unloading a van. Hastily, she arranged her scowling features into a smile, but that made him blanch, so she guessed it wasn't an improvement. He probably thought she was deranged.

Scuttling past, she carried on with her walk, grimacing when she caught sight of herself in the window of the cafe. With her unbrushed hair, red cheeks and wild expression, she looked positively manic.

Which was why she needed a dog. No one looked twice at someone taking a dog for a walk at seven-thirty in the morning, but a lone, middle-aged, overweight female trying to power-walk down the high street made people look twice. She suspected it was because they couldn't believe their eyes.

Of course, she'd probably have to make the walk a bit longer when she had Biscuit in tow, but at least this was a start.

On her return home, Nora peeled off her leggings and tee shirt and stood in her bathroom clad only in her underwear, and eyed the scales. Should she weigh herself again or was she becoming obsessed?

She got on the scales.

Ah, *that* was more like it, she thought, and let out an exuberant cry. She'd lost three pounds! The restrictive, boring, tasteless diet she was on was finally bearing fruit. Not that she could actually *eat* much fruit. For one thing, she wasn't keen on it, and for another, it was high in sugar.

But the thought of something sweet made her tastebuds tingle.

Stop it, she told herself, stripping off her bra and knickers and getting in the shower. She couldn't risk giving in to her craving because she was doing so well. The difficulty was keeping it up: but now that she could see she was making progress, she had renewed resolve.

She could do this. And having Biscuit was going to be an enormous help.

ELIJAH TOOK A BATCH of miniature banana bread loaves out of the oven and slid them onto a wire rack to cool. On autopilot, he reached for the industrial sized food mixer and pulled it closer, ready to receive the ingredients he'd pre-weighed for the next thing he was about to bake. But as he worked, he wasn't thinking about what he was doing – he was thinking about his love rival.

Nora had popped into his mind because he'd stuck his head into the shop earlier and had spotted her striding along the high street with a face like thunder. He'd ducked back into the kitchen and thankfully she hadn't seen him, but she'd been on his mind ever since.

Ah, who was he kidding? She'd been on his mind since Monday when he'd discovered that they were both interested in the same dog, and even more so since yesterday.

For all Nora's confident bluster, there was a certain vulnerability about her, and he wondered what her story was.

'I saw Nora Bunting earlier,' he said to Andrea when he went into the shop again. 'What do you know about her?' He wasn't entirely sure what he was fishing for. Aside from knowing she owned the hairdressing salon and she lived in the village, he didn't know a great deal. He'd never been one for gossip and he tended to keep himself to himself. If running wasn't involved, Elijah generally wasn't interested.

'What do you mean?' Andrea asked, then a slow smile spread across her face.

'Don't read anything into it,' he warned. 'I'm asking because she wants to adopt the same dog I want to adopt.' Andrea continued to stare at him, so he gave her a brief explanation, finishing with, 'I just wondered what kind of person she is.'

'Trying to find some mud to sling? Like, is she a secret cat lover and wants to adopt a dog to give her kitties something to sharpen their claws on?' she teased.

'Now you're being daft.' Elijah pulled a face.

As she served the next customer, she replied, 'She's been doing my hair for years. I like her. She's down to earth, fun, the life and soul of the party. She's *nice*.'

Elijah suspected Nora might be. However, it wasn't what he wanted to hear. He'd hoped she was horrid, so he could feel better about depriving her of the dog she'd set her heart on.

Andrea continued, 'I've heard she's on a bit of a health kick, which is why she hasn't been in for a while, but I didn't realise she was thinking of getting a dog.'

Elijah reminded her, 'She's not just thinking, she's applied for the same dog *I've* applied for.' He tapped his chest indignantly.

'Surely there are other dogs that need loving homes? Can't you pick one of those?'

'Can't *she*?' he retorted. 'Biscuit is a big dog with lots of energy. She'd be better suited to something smaller, especially since she's going to take it to work with her.' He gritted his teeth.

That factor could be a deal breaker, and there wasn't a damn thing he could do about it.

'AGILITY,' ELIJAH announced as soon as he saw Jakob later that afternoon. To his annoyance, Nora had arrived at the kennels before him. She'd clearly walked from the village too, as she appeared to be as hot and bothered as when he'd seen her on the high street this morning. More so, since she was clutching a water bottle and breathing hard.

Ironically, *he* was the one who'd driven to Muddypuddle Lane today as he hadn't wanted to be late, because there'd been a last-minute issue with an overflowing sink (his fault, he hadn't been paying attention) that he'd had to deal with.

'Agility,' Jakob echoed blankly.

'Do you think Biscuit will be any good at it? Because I thought I'd enrol him in a class. You know, give him some mental as well as physical stimulation. I noticed that there's one of those tunnels that's used in agility competitions in the field.' Elijah was hoping he could make up for having to leave the dog for a few hours every morning by making the rest of his life super fun.

How much fun was the poor animal going to get in a hairdressing salon? Okay, Biscuit wouldn't be on his own, but neither would he be doing anything *doggy*. Elijah knew which he would prefer if he were a dog, and it wouldn't be lying in a stuffy salon surrounded by hairdryers and gossipy women.

Jakob said, 'I think you ought to hold fire for a while before you sign up for anything.' Which Elijah translated as "you need to wait and see whether you're chosen to re-home him".

It pained him to acknowledge that the man was right. Elijah *was* getting ahead of himself. However, his comment kind of served its purpose when he noticed the flash of concern on Nora's face, and he hoped she was having second thoughts about taking the dog on. Elijah had been honest when he'd told Andrea that he thought a smaller dog would be better for Nora. And once again, he told himself that if he honestly didn't believe *he* was the most suitable owner for Biscuit, he would bow out.

Although Elijah wasn't entirely sure how true that was, because when he looked into Biscuit's intelligent brown eyes once more, he felt his heart constrict.

Once again, Jakob took them to the field and let them play with Biscuit for an hour or so. This time Nora had also brought some treats, and Elijah was ready with the ball. So when Biscuit had been given a few, Elijah began to toss the ball in the air, catching the dog's attention.

For a while Biscuit was torn. Ball or treat? Treat or ball?

The ball won, but not completely, because after every third or fourth throw, he'd trot over to Nora and stare at her with a pleading look to beg for another morsel.

To Elijah, it seemed as though the dog's favourite human was whoever happened to have what he wanted at the time. Biscuit was showing no particular preference for one or the other of them, although Elijah was still convinced there was a connection between him and the dog that Nora didn't have. He just needed her to see it, but at the moment, he had no idea how he could make that happen.

THE NEXT DAY saw Nora in a foul mood, although she was trying not to show it. It wasn't Kendra's fault that today was her day off and that Paige was covering for her, meaning Nora couldn't possibly leave the salon this afternoon. She was needed *here*, which left Elijah free to see Biscuit all on his own.

She felt like growling with frustration, but what could she do? She just had to trust that Biscuit wouldn't be swayed by Elijah's cloying attention.

As morning became afternoon, Nora found herself becoming more and more tense, to the point where she lost focus once or twice. Thankfully it didn't happen when she was snipping anyone's hair, but the fact it had happened at all was concerning.

Would Biscuit wonder where she was? Probably not. Nora was being silly, projecting human thoughts and feelings onto the dog. However, Elijah would be expecting her to turn up at any moment, then he'd be exultant when he realised she wasn't coming.

Although Nora guessed that her not being at the kennels today would make little difference to Dawn's eventual decision, she nevertheless felt as though she was giving Elijah an advantage. And when Andrea popped in to make an appointment for a cut and colour, it kind of added insult to injury.

'I hear you and Elijah have set your sights on the same dog,' Andrea began.

'Apparently so.' Nora had known Andrea for years, but she felt suddenly wary. Was the woman here to spy on her? 'Has he gone to the kennels this afternoon?' she asked.

'He has; Christina and Olive are manning the fort. Smitten with that dog, he is.'

Nora ground her teeth together as she consulted the diary. 'When were you thinking of? I'm fully booked next week, but I can do the week after.'

'How about the Wednesday?'

Nora pencilled her name in. 'All booked,' she said, expecting Andrea to leave now that she'd made an appointment, but the woman continued to linger.

'Have you heard that Elijah has been told he shouldn't run anymore? Poor love, he's really down at the moment. I really feel for him. He lives for his running.'

Yes, Nora had heard, and he had seemed rather upset when he'd mentioned on

Monday that he used to run marathons. 'It's a shame,' she said, and was about to sympathise further when a thought occurred to her. 'Did *he* put you up to this?'

'Up to what?'

'Trying to make me feel sorry for him so I'll withdraw my application to adopt Biscuit?'

Andrea's eyes widened. 'Of course not!'

Nora didn't believe her, and frankly she was dismayed but not totally surprised to discover that he'd stooped so low.

For a second, she was tempted to blurt out her own circumstances, but she kept her counsel; the last thing she wanted was anyone, least of all Elijah, feeling sorry for *her*.

ELIJAH KEPT GLANCING towards the gate, expecting to see Nora hurrying towards it, but when half-past two came and went and she still hadn't appeared, he began to wonder where she was. Had something happened to delay her? Was she (he prayed this was indeed the case) having second thoughts about adopting Biscuit?

Elijah wasn't about to complain that she wasn't here, though – he was enjoying having the dog to himself far too much. Without Nora to distract him, Biscuit gave Elijah his full attention, and Elijah revelled in it. But after an hour of entertaining the dog on his own, he felt restless. He wasn't built for standing still, and he longed to be able to take Biscuit for a walk, so when he spotted Jakob, he called him over.

'Do you think I could walk him?' he asked, and was delighted when Jakob agreed, with the proviso that Elijah didn't let him off the lead.

Elijah was more than happy with that. In fact, he was over the moon he was being allowed to take Biscuit out and didn't have to share this first precious walk with Nora.

However, it surprised him to discover he felt a little guilty. He knew she'd be disappointed and maybe even a tad upset, but it was hardly his fault she wasn't here, was it? Then again, if she'd decided not to go ahead with her adoption bid, it didn't matter a fig, so he told himself to enjoy the walk. Which he did, but part of him, a part which up to now he hadn't known existed, missed her company.

Maybe he'd call in to the salon later and check she was okay? He'd hate to be gloating over his good fortune if something was wrong.

'**EXCUSE THE PLAY** on words, but you take the biscuit,' Nora spat, and Elijah took a step back in surprise.

He'd done as he'd intended and had popped in on his way home from The Forever Home to check on her. She'd certainly looked okay, since she'd been standing behind a lady who was seated in front of a mirror, with a comb in one hand and a pair of scissors in the other, and had been chatting away. She'd looked animated and lively, less pale and drawn than recently, and it was nice to see her smiling.

Unfortunately, when she glanced at the door to see who'd entered, the smile was instantly replaced by incredulity, quickly followed by ire, and he wondered how she'd found out about him taking Biscuit for a walk. Had she phoned the kennels to check how his visit had gone?

'That was *so* underhand,' she snapped.

Elijah shook his head in disbelief. She was being so unreasonable.

'Anyway, what do you want?' she demanded, her eyes flashing fire.

Crossly he said, 'Nothing. It doesn't matter.' No way was he going to admit he'd called in because he was concerned about her – a concern that was clearly misplaced. There was nothing wrong with Nora Bunting that a good dose of manners couldn't put right.

Angrily, he turned on his heel, but before he left, he called over his shoulder, 'By the way, Biscuit had a lovely time on his walk. He didn't miss you at all.'

Then he stomped out, Nora's furious expression as she stared after him, emblazoned on his mind.

CHAPTER NINE

THE ATMOSPHERE IN the field at The Forever Home the following day was cold enough to be mistaken for the Arctic. Neither Nora nor Elijah had spoken to each other since they'd arrived, and the air was thick with tension.

Nora might be childish, but she was trying to pretend Elijah didn't exist. Which wasn't easy, since she was acutely aware of every move he made and every word he uttered. Not to *her*, obviously, but first to Jakob and then to Biscuit.

'I believe it's *my* turn to take Biscuit for a walk,' she told Jakob. 'Since *he—*' She frowned at Elijah '— took him out yesterday.'

Elijah was quick to say, 'If you'd been here, you could have come with us. It's not my fault you missed it.'

'Some of us had to work,' she shot back, then wished she hadn't when Elijah gave Jakob a significant look, as though to say that *he* hadn't had to. Just in time, she remembered she was the one who'd be able to take Biscuit to work, so she swiftly added, 'Luckily, he can come the salon with *me*, so it doesn't matter if I have to work or not – unlike *some* people I could mention. So, about that walk?'

Jakob rolled his eyes and muttered something which sounded like, 'Give me strength', but Nora couldn't be certain. 'You can take him if you want,' he said.

Nora clapped her hands in glee. 'Yay!'

'Together,' Jakob clarified, and it was Elijah's turn to look pleased.

Jakob's expression was stern. 'Do you think you can manage to take him for a walk without squabbling? Because if you can't...' He glared at them, his warning clear.

Nora felt remarkably like a child who'd just been scolded by a teacher. Contrite, she promised, 'We won't squabble,' and followed it up with a meaningful glower at Elijah.

The way they were carrying on, they were risking not being able to see Biscuit at all, and maybe not even being allowed to adopt him. She, for one, wasn't prepared to let that happen, even if Elijah *was* an underhand sneaky scumbag.

His expression was apologetic, and he nodded his agreement. He even went as far as to step back when Jakob held out Biscuit's lead so she could hold it.

Nora wasn't taken in, though; he was only doing it to look good in front of Jakob, and she guessed he was still hoping Jakob might favour him when (or even *if*) Dawn canvassed her colleague's opinion. Elijah wasn't taking any chances. And neither should she.

Determined to take full advantage of this opportunity, Nora wrapped the lead around her fist and set off. Biscuit fell into step, walking nicely by her side, and as long as she stared straight ahead, she could pretend Elijah wasn't with her.

Until he started speaking and she couldn't pretend any longer.

'How's the walking coming along?' he asked.

'Why do you want to know?'

'Just making conversation.'

'Well, don't.' Nora came to a halt at the entrance to The Forever Home and glanced up and down the road, wondering which way to go. Left would lead them back down Muddypuddle Lane, right would take them across the top of the mountain and the scrubby moorland. Despite having lived in Picklewick all her life, she'd rarely ventured up this way.

Elijah sensed her hesitation. 'That way,' he suggested, pointing to the right. 'I go – *used to go* – running around here. The track drops down into the trees and circles around. It'll take about—' He hesitated, glancing at her out of the corner of his eye. '—an hour.'

She bristled, hoping he wasn't insinuating that she mightn't be able to walk that far, but all she said was, 'Perfect.'

They set off in silence again, Nora once more determined to ignore him, but she found her resolution flagging as Biscuit kept stopping to sniff, or bounced around on the end of his lead. He was clearly enjoying being out and about, with different sights and new smells, and when he paused to sniff enthusiastically at a clump of ferns and then started to dig through them as he made little grunting noises of excitement, she couldn't help giggling.

'I wonder if he's trying to dig out a rabbit?' she said, watching his antics in amusement, momentarily forgetting that the man standing next to her was her rival.

'I bet he won't catch it if he does,' Elijah said. 'It'll be far too quick for him.' He froze and lowered his voice, pointing. 'Look, there's a squirrel.'

Nora looked, but couldn't see anything. 'Where?'

Elijah moved nearer until his shoulder was touching her, and he leant in, his head close to hers. 'Follow my finger,' he said. 'Just there, between those two trees. Do you see it?'

The bushy grey tail curved over its back as the squirrel sat on the ground, holding something in its tiny paws. Motionless, it watched them with black beady eyes.

Nora sucked in a slow, awed breath – and her nose was immediately filled with the scent of cinnamon and sugar, with an undercurrent of sandalwood and bergamot. She was sure she could smell coconut and vanilla, too. The man smelt good enough to eat, and she closed her eyes briefly, letting the aroma seep into her, reminding her of cookies and biscuits, cakes and pastries, and she had to fight the temptation to turn her head and find out whether he tasted as delicious as he smelt.

Abruptly coming to her senses, she leapt away in alarm. What the hell was she *doing?*

'You okay?' he asked, concern in his eyes.

'Wasp,' she blurted, saying the first thing to come into her head. At least it was plausible.

'Where?' His eyes darted about.

'It's gone now.'

'Good. I hate wasps.'

'Me, too.' She tugged at Biscuit's lead and he ceased scrabbling in the undergrowth, to look at her with an inquisitive expression. 'Come on,' she said. 'This is supposed to be a walk, not a dig.'

Feeling rather shaken, she carried on, wondering what had just happened. For crying out loud, she'd wanted to *kiss* him! And all because he'd reminded her of the smell of cake.

She really had to stop thinking about all the food she could no longer eat, and she put her bizarre reaction down to the fact that he baked sweet treats for a living, so the aroma of sugar was probably ingrained in his pores. It had been nothing more than a desire to eat cake, and not a desire to eat *him*.

He was very attractive though, she acknowledged, but that aside, she wasn't interested. It had been a very long time since she'd had a man in her life, and she didn't need one now. She certainly didn't feel the lack and was perfectly content being on her own. Anyway, she wouldn't be on her own for much longer: Biscuit would soon be moving in, and she couldn't wait.

Feeling magnanimous because Elijah was going to be one disappointed chappie when he discovered that Nora would be Biscuit's new human, she thrust the lead at him. 'Your turn.'

'Are you sure?' He looked startled; as well he might, considering the way he'd behaved yesterday. He clearly hadn't been expecting any favours. Ha! That showed him! She was the bigger person, even though she was still smarting from the way he'd sent Andrea to play on her sympathies. But it had been the sign of a desperate man, and she took comfort from it.

Nora shrugged and thrust the lead at him again. This time he took it with a grateful smile, and she felt bad that he wouldn't get to take Biscuit home; but not *too* bad. After all, her need was greater than his. Okay, so he'd had to give up running, but he'd find something else to occupy his time, whereas Nora's health depended on her losing weight and keeping it off, and along with her strict diet, exercise would play a key role in ensuring that happened. She wasn't getting a dog for fun (although she was sure Biscuit would bring joy and companionship into her life), and neither was she doing it on a whim. This was survival – emotional as well as physical, because in the short time she'd known Biscuit, she'd fallen head over heels in love with the daft pooch. He'd filled a dog-shaped hole in her heart that she hadn't even known was there.

But now that she did, no other dog would do.

Biscuit was her soul dog, and she had an awful suspicion that if she wasn't allowed to adopt him, it would break her heart in two.

ELIJAH WAS NONPLUSSED! Nora was being nice to him. Also, for a second, when he'd been pointing out the squirrel to her, he'd had the weirdest feeling she'd been about to *kiss* him.

And what was even more worrying was that he'd wanted her to.

The woman was getting under his skin, and it made him uncomfortable. Fancying Nora wasn't a good idea, and not just because they were in the middle of battling for the affection of the same dog. It was the main reason, of course, but there were others. They were complete opposites, for a start. He loved the outdoors and, from what he'd gathered, she wasn't as keen, despite her newfound intentions. He was a bit of a loner, and she was the life and soul of the party. He didn't want another relationship and she— Actually, he didn't know *what* she wanted.

Anyway, it made no difference to him, because whatever it was, he didn't care enough to find out. He simply wasn't interested.

'Have you always been a hairdresser?' he asked, blurting out the question before he realised he was going to ask it. Huh! So much for him not being interested!

Surprise flickered across her face. 'Yes. Have you always been a baker?'

'I have, actually. Got interested in baking at school. A Victoria sponge.'

She smiled. 'I had a toy head for Christmas when I was six.'

'A what?' Elijah blinked.

'It's a doll's head with hair you can style.'

'Just the *head*?'

She nodded.

'Gruesome.'

Her laughter rang out. 'I suppose it is, but I loved it. I've been playing with hair ever since.'

'Andrea tells me you've always lived in Picklewick.'

'Ah, yes, *Andrea*.' Her voice was frosty and the atmosphere took a sudden nosedive.

Elijah had no idea why. 'Is something wrong?'

'You could say that. I don't appreciate you sending your staff around to play the sympathy card on your behalf.'

'I'm sorry... What?'

'Please don't insult my intelligence by pretending you don't know what I'm talking about.'

'I don't.'

Nora snorted in disbelief and came to a halt. Putting her hands on her hips, she pressed her lips together. Biscuit whined, sensing the tension. Elijah glanced at him, concerned, however Nora ignored the dog. She was on a roll about something, but Elijah had no clue what.

'Andrea,' Nora said slowly, as though spelling out the syllables to a child.

Perplexed, Elijah asked, 'What about her?'

'She was in the salon yesterday.'

'So?' Andrea had told him she'd been getting her hair done there for years, so what was unusual about her going to the salon?

Nora was shaking her head, anger flashing in her eyes. 'As you well know, she tried to get me to change my mind about adopting Biscuit by trying to make me feel sorry for you. I mean, I do – a bit – but that's beside the point. You're not the only person with problems. Maybe you should think about that!'

Biscuit whined again as she huffed and strode past them up the path.

Elijah was conflicted. Should he go after her and plead his innocence, or should he let her go and give her time to cool off?

Remembering Jakob's warning and recalling that his own default setting of conflict avoidance hadn't helped in the past, Elijah decided to go after her. Biscuit seemed to agree, because he was pulling on the lead and whining pitifully, while shooting Elijah anxious, pleading glances. His tail and his ears were down, and his worry was evident.

'You're not happy, are you, boy? I'll let you into a secret – neither am I. Come on, let's go catch her up.'

When he fell into step next to Nora, Biscuit nudged her on the leg, forcing her to slow down and acknowledge him.

She halted briefly to stroke the dog's ears, then carried on walking.

'Nora, listen to me,' Elijah urged. 'I don't know what Andrea said to you, but I didn't put her up to it. In fact, I'm rather annoyed she said anything to you at all. It's nothing to do with her. I'll have a word with her in the morning,' he added crossly.

Nora stopped. 'Please don't. I'm sure she was merely looking out for you.'

Elijah wasn't mollified. 'I don't need looking out for. And you've changed your tune. I thought you'd be happy that I didn't have anything to do with it.'

'I am. But I don't want to get Andrea into trouble.' She looked so worried that Elijah's ire subsided. Andrea shouldn't have said anything, but he believed she had his best interests at heart. He would still have a word, but it would be a gentle one.

When Biscuit let out a bark, it made both him and Nora jump, and Elijah chuckled at the dog's transformation: his tail was up once more, and his whole demeanour had lifted. He even looked as though he was smiling.

'I don't think he likes it when we squabble,' Nora observed.

'No, I don't think he does either, so it's best we don't, isn't it?' He held out a hand for her to shake. 'Friends?'

Nora laughed. 'I wouldn't go that far. Frenemies, more like.'

'Frenemies it is.' But when her hand slipped into his, the spark that travelled up his arm at her touch, ignited something in his chest.

He liked her, he realised. And not only that, he desired her, too.

Oh, dear, this wasn't going to end well, was it?

CHAPTER TEN

NORA GAZED AT THE menu in dismay, trying to find something tasty that wasn't either loaded with carbs or wasn't a sodding salad. And she was sick to bloody death of vegetables. Right now, she didn't think she could eat another stick of celery or floret of broccoli without throwing up. Yet here she was, sitting around a table with Trinny and some of Trinny's friends from work, in a gastro pub in Thornbury on a Saturday evening, contemplating an effin' bowl of leaves.

It made her stomach churn. It also made her want to cry.

'Go on,' someone urged. 'Let your hair down. You can go back on the diet tomorrow. Aren't you allowed cheat meals?'

Nora kept her eyes glued to the menu and muttered a non-committal, 'Hmm.'

Trinny said, 'You can eat anything in moderation, Nora.'

Nora glared at her. Trinny should know better, since she knew the reason.

'It's true,' Trinny insisted. 'I've been reading...' She ground to a halt and bit her lip.

'I've heard that the keto diet is the way to go,' someone else said. 'I keep meaning to try it, but I like bread too much. I'd die if I had to give up bread. And pasta. I couldn't live without pasta.'

'What about chips? Hot, salty, vinegary chips. Mmm.'

'Oh, yes, chips. I forgot about those. You can't not have chips.'

You can, Nora thought, *when you don't have any choice.* And surprisingly, people don't die if they don't eat bread or pasta. She was proof of that – although, right now, she felt as though life wasn't worth living. She couldn't go on like this.

Scanning the menu again in the hope of finding something to get her tastebuds tingling, Nora wished she hadn't agreed to come out this evening. She just about had a handle on her boring food at home, but being here was testing her resolve.

No matter how often she read that getting a grip on diabetes was a marathon and not a sprint, and that she needed to be kind to herself and not to make too many changes at once, she was terrified what might happen if she didn't get her blood glucose under control.

'Imagine a life without chocolate?' the woman on Trinny's left said, and Nora felt like pushing her off her chair – because Nora wasn't *imagining* it, she was *living* it, and chocolate was the thing she missed the most.

Maybe she'd have the butternut squash soup? But that was a starter, so would it be weird if she ordered it for her main? And was butternut squash considered a carby vegetable?

Oh, sod it. One meal wouldn't hurt, and she'd been really good since her diagnosis. 'I'll have the focaccia with balsamic vinegar, olives and sun-dried tomato to start, followed by the burger with Monterey Jack cheese and triple cooked chips,' she decided. She'd even have a dessert after, if she felt like it. If she was going to fall off the healthy eating wagon, she may as well do it in style: there was no point in half-measures.

And when Trinny offered to top up her wineglass, Nora didn't object. She would simply have to go on an ultra-long walk tomorrow to burn off all the extra calories she would consume this evening.

THE HANGOVER (if that's what it was) began even before Nora arrived home that evening. Or maybe it was something she'd eaten? The burger, perhaps?

It started with feeling nauseous, then a stomach ache followed, accompanied by a headache. Wearily, feeling like death warmed up, Nora collapsed into bed, exhausted. Then she felt so thirsty she could drink the Atlantic dry, so she had to fetch another glass of water. But of course, what goes in, must come out, so she couldn't get to sleep because she needed to pee every five minutes. Not only that, she seemed to have been lying awkwardly, because she kept getting a kind of pins and needles in her toes, like a burning sensation, which saw her stick both feet out of the bottom of the bedcovers in the hope it would cool her trotters.

Things finally seemed to settle down after a while, and she was gratefully drifting off to sleep and thankful she didn't have to get up for work in the morning, when an odd and uncomfortable fluttering in her chest made her sit up.

Bloody hell, that was all she needed – palpitations. She used to get them quite often, but since she'd stopped drinking so much cola and coffee, they'd eased off.

Come to think about it, she hadn't had any for a couple of weeks, so why was she having them *now* when she hadn't consumed any caffeine at all this evening?

Nora switched on the bedside lamp and took a deep breath. Then realised that the vision in her one eye was blurry again.

Oh hell; she had a feeling she knew what was going on, but without being able to test her glucose levels (should she invest in a monitor?) she couldn't be a hundred per cent certain.

This wasn't a hangover, she suspected, but it *was* probably due to what she'd consumed, because she'd dumped a shed load of carbs into her system.

Panicking a little, she squinted one-eyed at her phone as she typed in what she could do about it.

Drink loads of water to try to help flush the excess sugar out of her bloodstream and do some exercise was the advice, so Nora got dressed, slipped her feet into some trainers, grabbed her water bottle, and headed out the door.

This was ridiculous, she thought, as she marched through the dark streets. This wasn't what she should be doing at one o'clock in the morning. And on her own, too. If she'd had Biscuit with her, she wouldn't feel quite so ridiculous. Or nervous.

Despite having lived in Picklewick all her life and knowing most of its residents (by sight, if not personally), Nora was tense and jittery. Anyone could be about. And as she walked around a corner, she realised how true that was, when she saw the unmistakable figure of Elijah Grant running towards her.

Startled, she stopped walking and her mouth dropped open. Elijah was almost upon her before he realised she was there and, equally surprised, he skidded to a halt.

'What are you—?' she began, at the same time he said, 'Why are you—?'

'You first,' he said. A streetlamp illuminated his face, and as he flexed his leg, she noticed him wincing.

'I didn't think you were supposed to be running,' she accused, suspecting he'd been playing her, because, unless she was very much mistaken, running was precisely what he was doing.

'I'm not.' His expression was sheepish. 'I couldn't sleep, and I got to thinking...' He trailed off.

'You wanted to see if you still could?' she guessed sympathetically. Hadn't she kind of done the same thing herself tonight?

He nodded.

'It looks like you can,' she said, a seed of hope beginning to germinate. If he could run again, would that mean he'd no longer want to adopt Biscuit?

'Yeah,' he agreed. He didn't seem happy about it, though.

'But?'

'It hurts.' His admission was stark, accompanied by a tightening of the lips.

'Does that mean...?'

'That I definitely won't be running anymore? I'm afraid so.'

'You were hoping they'd got it wrong, weren't you?'

'Wouldn't you?' His gaze was level.

That was *exactly* what she was hoping when it came to her own diagnosis, but she hadn't been prepared to take the risk. She was due another blood test in a little over two months, and she was praying that her "number" would have gone down, and that her diabetes would be in remission. Maybe she was also hoping that her GP would say, 'Sorry, we made a mistake, you're not diabetic after all', even though she knew that would never happen,

'Anyway,' Elijah said, 'why are you walking the streets in the middle of the night?'

'Couldn't sleep,' she replied truthfully. 'I ate a really heavy meal earlier,' she added, also truthfully.

'Been out long?'

'Ten minutes.'

'How much longer are you planning on staying out?'

Probably until she needed another wee. She shrugged. 'Until I feel tired.' Not true: she felt tired now, but she couldn't work out whether it was genuine tiredness or because her body wanted to slip into a food coma.

'Fancy some company?' he asked.

'Shouldn't you go home and rest your leg?'

'Maybe, but I don't want to. I'm still wide awake.'

'Okay, then.' She carried on walking, and Elijah joined her.

The streets were empty and quiet, with few lights on in the houses they passed, and no cars or people. There was a cat, a ginger tom who stood his ground on the pavement, forcing them to walk around him, and Nora silently acknowledged that the night was his domain, not hers. As they passed underneath a streetlight, a bat flitted overhead chasing down the moths drawn to the glow. In the distance a fox barked, and she shivered.

She was glad to have Elijah by her side and they walked in companionable silence for a while, until Elijah broke it.

'What did you eat earlier to make you so restless?' he asked.

'A three-course meal with wine. Since I've been... on this diet, I'm not used to eating that amount of food.' She'd nearly slipped up there, but caught herself in time.

'You can't fool me,' he said, giving her the side-eye. 'I know what's really going on.'

'Oh?' Nora tensed. How could he – unless Kendra had blabbed?

'You're getting into training ready for walking Biscuit.'

Some of the tension flowed out of her. 'Can't resist a dig, can you?'

'It wasn't a dig. I was teasing.' He paused. 'Sorry.' Another pause, then he said, 'Where did you go for your meal?'

'A gastro pub in Thornbury.'

'Was it any good?'

'It was lovely.'

'I'll have to try it sometime, though to be honest, I don't eat out often.'

Neither would Nora from now on. 'Do you get fed up of food, since you're surrounded by it all day?'

'Not really, although I wouldn't usually order a pastry out. Too much like a busman's holiday.'

'You're from Thornbury originally, aren't you?'

'That's right.'

'How do you like living in Picklewick?'

'I love it.'

'We don't see you around much.'

'We?' He raised his eyebrows and Nora blushed.

'It's a turn of phrase,' she said. 'What I mean is, *I* never see you in The Black Horse, or in the shop, for that matter. You're always out the back.'

'That's where the magic happens. You said you're one of my best customers?'

Nora hesitated. 'I was.'

'But not anymore?' His expression was teasing. 'What can I do to tempt you back?'

'I'm on a diet, remember?' Her tone was sharper than she'd intended, but she was getting a little fed up with people trying to persuade her that "one won't hurt".

'You're really serious about losing weight, aren't you?'

'So?' she retorted belligerently.

He said softly, 'I think you're perfect as you are.'

The way he said it made her heart flutter, an entirely different sensation to the one that had driven her from her bed earlier. But no less disturbing.

So it was fortuitous that she was almost home.

Hurrying to her front door, she said, 'This is me. Thanks for keeping me company.'

'My pleasure.'

The problem Nora had when she gently shut the door as he strolled away, was that he'd sounded as though he'd meant it.

And she'd enjoyed it, too.

CHAPTER ELEVEN

ELIJAH WOKE ON Sunday morning with three things on his mind. The first – that there was no doubt he would never run again – didn't come as a shock. The second, that it would be another week before Dawn, the sanctuary's manager, would consider his application, was met with resignation.

The third was that he was looking forward to seeing Nora today.

It was this which concerned him the most, because the last time he'd looked forward to spending time with a woman, he'd married her and it hadn't ended well.

Which was probably why he'd been single since the divorce.

He'd had many first dates, but few had led to second ones, and only once in twelve years had he got as far as date number three. There simply hadn't been a spark.

But Nora was different. He couldn't put his finger on how or why. She just was.

When he'd seen her last night, he'd been surprised at first, then mildly alarmed. Was her quest to lose weight so important to her that she had to roam the streets in the middle of the night? Seeing her alone in the darkness had given him the shivers, and he'd been relieved when she'd agreed to let him accompany her, and even more relieved when he'd safely delivered her to her door. He'd also meant it when he'd told her she was perfect the way she was, although he couldn't believe he'd actually said it out loud. What a muppet.

The bakery wasn't open on Sundays, but this morning Elijah felt an unexpected urge to play with dough, to bake something different, and not because he wanted to produce a new product to improve sales (although that would be welcome), but for the sheer act of baking something new.

It had been a long time since he'd felt like baking for the love of it.

He never baked at home these days, wanting to keep his work life separate, but there'd once been a time when the house – the one he'd shared with his wife and son – had been rich with the smell of fresh bread, the air seeded with a fine dusting of flour or icing sugar. A time when he'd been happy...

Elijah sighed, pushing aside the dreary memories of his failed marriage, and with it the desire to bake.

He'd go for a run instead— Ah, no, he wouldn't be doing that, either: the deep ache in his leg last night had been a warning, and one he would be foolish to ignore.

Another walk, then?

But walking on his own was a different kettle of fish to *running* on his own. Running was purposeful. Walking was...?

Second best.

Elijah slumped in his living room chair feeling restless, useless, adrift. On any normal Sunday, he'd be halfway through a fifteen-mile run by now and thoroughly enjoying every step. At least if he had a dog he could—

His thoughts turned to Biscuit.

A big dog like that needed a lot of exercise. Bernese Mountain Dogs had been bred to herd cattle in the Swiss Alps, and they'd also been used to pull small carts to transport cheeses. They liked being active (he'd been reading up on them) and he'd be more than happy to give Biscuit the exercise needed. He certainly wouldn't be sitting in an armchair contemplating his navel if he had Biscuit to care for; he'd be out on the hillside, putting in the miles.

Restlessly he picked up his phone, remembered he'd deleted the RunMad app, and put it down again, a crushing loneliness assailing him. It was pathetic that he missed people he only really knew via an electronic device, that those usernames had been his only social life and without them he felt lost.

The sole light in the gloom of his self-pity was the prospect of adopting Biscuit.

And seeing Nora at the kennels this afternoon.

WHAT WAS I THINKING, was Nora's first thought when she opened her eyes to a bright and sunny Sunday morning.

Was it morning?

She checked: only just. There was enough time for a shower and some brunch before she needed to set off for The Forever Home and her rendezvous with Biscuit. And Elijah, because he would no doubt be there.

Thinking of Elijah brought her smartly back to questioning her own sanity.

What had she been thinking, traipsing around Picklewick in the middle of the night? She should have stayed at home and done a hundred star jumps or something.

She hadn't been thinking at all. She'd been panicking. At least she felt okay this morning, and as she tucked into a three-egg omelette a short while later, she vowed never to be as silly again. No more pigging out on foods that she knew weren't good for her, and no more midnight walks.

Not on her own, anyway. It was lucky it was Elijah she'd bumped into and not some weirdo.

She wondered how he was feeling today. Not good, she suspected. He'd looked defeated last night, and her heart went out to him. Despite not being able to understand his passion for running, she could sympathise. Her world had also been turned upside down recently.

When a cloud of self-pity threatened to loom over her, Nora blew it away with a determined huff. She wasn't going to let this thing, this *condition*, define her. The meal out last night was simply part of the new learning curve she was on, as she worked out how to live with it. Just focus on getting the weight off, she told herself, as she locked her front door and set out. On foot, obviously.

Rather than walking along the main road, then turning off it to go up Muddypuddle Lane, Nora aimed for a kissing gate on the outskirts of the village, beyond which was a path leading through some fields that belonged to the stables. It was a far gentler and prettier walk up the hill than traversing the lane itself, which was quite steep, and since she was determined to walk it, the gentler the incline the better. Until she was a bit fitter, anyway. Hopefully, with Biscuit as an incentive to get her out the door, it wouldn't be too long before she was bounding up hills and trotting down dales.

As soon as she squeezed through the kissing gate (she'd had to suck in her stomach), she paused for a moment to take in the scene.

The field rippled as the breeze waved through stalks of feathery grass, and here and there wildflowers bobbed and nodded as insects hummed, buzzing busily from bloom to bloom.

A sense of peace settled over her. Why hadn't she done this more often, she asked herself, tilting her face to the sun and closing her eyes. The rays were warm on her cheeks and if she'd had time she would have sunk down into the grass and stayed there for a while.

The neigh of a horse in the distance and the call of a bird overhead were the only sounds.

Until...

'Nora? Wait up.'

Nora opened her eyes to see Elijah walking briskly towards her, and her heart gave a lurch.

Tanned and slim, he strode effortlessly along the path, and she was hit by a desire so strong it stole her breath.

'Are you alright?' he asked, his blue eyes peering at her. 'You look like you've seen a ghost. I'm not that scary, am I?'

She cleared her throat. 'I'm fine,' she replied hoarsely. 'I didn't expect to see anyone up here, that's all. I thought I'd check it out in case—' She stopped, her cheeks colouring.

'In case you adopt Biscuit?' he finished, pursing his lips when she nodded.

He looked regretful that she'd mentioned it, but it was the truth and for a while she'd forgotten the *enemy* part in frenemy. He wasn't her friend, but under different circumstances she would have liked him to be. If she was honest, she would have liked him to be *more* than a friend.

Typical! She hadn't looked at or thought about a man in that way for quite some time, and it was Sod's Law that when she did fancy the pants off someone, they were sworn enemies.

No matter which of them ended up adopting Biscuit, the one wouldn't be able to forgive the other. At least, *she* wouldn't be able to forgive *him*, so it was probably safe to assume that Elijah would feel the same.

'Recovered from your midnight adventure?' he asked after a while, and Nora was glad of the change of topic.

'Have *you?*'

'My leg still aches.'

Was that another attempt to gain her sympathy? She said, 'Do you often run in the witching hour?'

'Not usually, but I couldn't settle, and whenever I can't settle, I run. I guess I'm going to have to walk instead, now. It could be the start of a midnight walking club.' His chuckle was regretful and sad.

'To be honest, I prefer to be tucked up in bed at midnight,' she replied. Not too long ago, she'd have preferred to be in a bar or a club.

Without warning, Nora suddenly felt very old, Like, *eighty* old. The speed at which the years were slipping by, she *would* be eighty before too long; the previous thirty had flown by so fast. Yet, conversely, her teenage years seemed like several lifetimes ago, and lately her body was taking great delight in reminding her that she was no longer a spring chicken.

There had been a time when she could have raced up this hill, all the way to the top, and barely be out of breath when she got there. Now though, she was puffing and panting like Thomas the Tank Engine on a bad day, and she was beginning to regret not driving up. She was already out of breath, her thighs were on fire, and she was sweating buckets – and they weren't even halfway there yet.

Elijah, damn him, looked as cool as a polar bear sitting on a glacier, and he didn't need to catch his breath because he hadn't lost it. He looked as though he was out for a saunter along the high street.

'I love this view,' he said, pausing and turning back to gaze at it, giving Nora the opportunity to take a breather.

God, she was so unfit.

Cross with herself, she quickly turned to continue the trudge up the hill, and promptly lost her footing on the uneven path. Her leg went from underneath her and she would have face-planted the ground if it hadn't been for Elijah's quick-fire reaction, as he grabbed her around the waist and pulled her towards him.

She came up against his chest with a thud that sent them both tumbling backwards.

Elijah juddered back a couple of paces, before regaining his balance.

 'Are you okay?' he asked. He still had hold of her and as she looked into his eyes, she could see the concern in them.

Nora, who prided herself on rarely crying, promptly burst into tears.

She didn't want to do this anymore.

She'd had her fill of being diabetic. She wanted everything to go back to the way it had been before she'd had the phone call from her GP.

It was so unfair.

'Are you hurt?' Elijah held her shoulders, searching her face for clues. 'Are you ill?'

'I'm fine,' she sobbed.

'Fine people don't cry.'

'It's nothing.' She was bawling now, her hands covering her face as she ugly cried big, fat tears.

'It's definitely *something*,' he persisted. 'What's wrong? Maybe I can help?'

'You can't.' He seriously couldn't, not when he smelled of vanilla and coconut, and reminded her of all the delicious things that were now out of bounds.

'Come here.' His voice was gentle as he drew her close and wrapped his arms around her.

Nora tensed, the gorgeous aroma intensifying. Then she slowly subsided into his embrace.

They stayed like that for a while, him holding her, and her snivelling until her tears ran their course and she managed to bring herself under control. When she disentangled herself, he silently handed her a tissue and she took it gratefully, blowing her nose.

'Sorry,' she muttered.

'Don't be. Better than keeping it bottled up. Is there anything I can do to help?' he asked again.

She gave him a wan smile. 'Relinquish your claim on Biscuit?'

'Apart from that.'

'No, then. But thank you for offering.'

'This isn't about Biscuit, is it?'

'Not really.'

'What is it?'

'Oh, you know, *life*.'

'Ah, *life*. Yep, you're right, I do know.'

'It can be a bugger sometimes.'

'Can't it just.'

Nora hitched in a breath. 'We're going to be late.'

'Are you sure you want to go to the kennels?'

'What, and let you have Biscuit all to yourself again? No chance!'

'I was going to offer to walk you home. Biscuit will still be there tomorrow.'

That was sweet of him, she thought.

Sweet? Why did everything come back to the one thing she could no longer have, she mused sadly. She might seriously have to consider changing Biscuit's name. Her smile came easier this time. 'Thank you, that's kind of you. I'm alright now, honestly. Let's push on, shall we?'

'If you're sure?' He sounded doubtful, and his eyes still held a hint of concern.

'I'm sure.' She uttered a self-conscious laugh. 'Don't worry, I won't sob all over you again.'

'I won't mind if you do.' He paused, then winced. 'Please don't take that the wrong way; I honestly don't want to see you cry. But if you do feel the need, then I'm your man. Mi shoulder es tu shoulder. Sorry, I don't know the Italian for shoulder.' He looked embarrassed. 'I'm babbling, aren't I?'

'It's better than sobbing.'

'You weren't sobbing; wailing a bit, maybe, but not sobbing.' He was smiling, but in a nice way.

He was actually a nice man.

More than nice.

Nora realised that she *really* liked him. A lot. *Shit.*

CHAPTER TWELVE

BISCUIT WAS AS delighted to see Elijah and Nora, as they were to see the dog. His tail was already wagging like mad as they approached his kennel, and when Elijah opened the door, Biscuit's back end nearly wagged itself off. He was uttering little whimpers of delight and dancing around, and Elijah laughed at his antics.

'I think someone is pleased to see us,' he said. 'Do you want to wrestle him into his harness, or shall I?'

'Wrestle is the right word for it,' Nora said. 'He gets so excited it's hard to put it on him, so you do it. I'll stand and watch you struggle.'

As though Biscuit knew what they were saying, he immediately calmed down and only danced a little when Elijah slipped the contraption over his head and hooked his front paws through.

'I swear he understands every word we say,' Elijah said, clipping the lead onto it and handing it to her. 'You can do the honours.'

It was as they were strolling away from the kennels, Nora holding the lead, the dog padding between them, it struck Elijah that they were acting like a couple taking their pooch for a walk. He felt comfortable with her, as though her being upset just now had breached a barrier between them, and had created a kind of bond. A silly notion really, since the barrier –

Biscuit – still separated them, literally and figuratively. How could he be friends with the woman who might take away the dog he had given his heart to?

Yet he felt closer to her now, and he wished he knew what she'd been upset about. Still *was* upset about, he sensed.

'Are you okay?' he asked, hoping she wouldn't think he was being overly solicitous or, worse, nosey.

'I will be.' She sounded determined.

'Men can be such bastards.' It was a stab in the dark, but relationships were often the cause of tears.

Nora's laugh was unexpected. 'It's not a man.' She gave him a sly look. 'Unless you're referring to yourself and your unreasonable determination not to let me have Biscuit.'

'That's unfair,' he said lightly. 'Anyway, my determination *isn't* unreasonable – I've fallen in love with him, just like you. Plus, I can give him a better home.' He grinned, to show there was no malice behind it.

'We're back to that, are we? In that case, who's going to look after him while you're at the bakery, hmm? No one, that's who. I'll have him with *me* all the time.'

'Not all the time, surely? What about when you want to go to the pub, or out for a meal or something?'

Was it his imagination or did her face cloud over? If it did, her expression quickly cleared as she retorted, 'The Black Horse is a dog-friendly establishment, and if dogs aren't welcome somewhere, then I won't go.'

'Damn it, I thought I had you there. Okay, I finish work at about one-thirty in the afternoon, so I can take him for humongous long walks afterwards.'

'*Humongous?* That far, eh?'

'I'm used to running marathons – for fun,' he added, doing a little jog on the spot to demonstrate and nearly losing his footing. Biscuit looked up at him with a "what *are* you doing" expression. The track over the mountain was uneven underfoot, rocky and gravel strewn, and Elijah recalled the many times he'd run across it without giving it a second thought – although it had always been a relief to reach the relative smoothness of Muddypuddle Lane, even if the tarmac was pitted with potholes.

'But you don't anymore,' she said softly, the breeze catching her words and whisking them away.

His mood took a downturn. 'No.'

Biscuit must have sensed it, because his tail took a downturn too, and he whined uncertainly. Elijah ruffled his ears. 'I'm okay, boy.'

'Are you?' Nora was studying him.

'I will be,' he echoed, with a wry twist of his lips. 'It's a big adjustment, not running anymore. I've been doing it for years, so to suddenly stop...' He stared into the distance, his mind not on the rolling moorland, nor the view over the valley, but on past runs where he'd felt strong and lithe, his feet eating the miles, his mind clear.

'Have you always run marathons?' she asked.

'Not at first. For years I used to run just to keep fit, but then you start getting into it, you know?'

Nora snorted. 'Not really. I refuse to even run for a bus.'

'I bet you used to run around when you were a child. Show me a kid that doesn't.'

'Me. I never liked sport.'

'Running isn't sport. Or, it doesn't have to be. It's just exercise, a way to keep the body moving and to not put on weight.'

'Never trust a skinny cook.' Her eyes were smiling.

'Unless they run ten miles every day, and then they've got a good reason to be skinny,' he rejoined.

'Is that why you do it?'

'I've never really thought about it. The two kind of went hand in hand. I used to bake because I enjoyed it, and I ran because I enjoy that, too.'

'It's no consolation, I know, but at least you can still bake.'

'Hmm...'

Her gaze turned to scrutiny. 'Don't you enjoy it anymore?'

She was perceptive, he realised. 'Not really.'

'Why not?'

Elijah shrugged. 'Life.'

'Hey, that's my line.'

He decided to be honest. 'I really don't know how it happened, but at some point, baking became just another job. Maybe when my marriage fell apart? I'm not totally sure. But it was all I knew how to do, and I was good at it, so...' He pulled a face.

'You still are.'

'Thanks.'

'I mean it. I'm not just saying it. I used to call in everyday for something.'

'But not anymore?'

'No...'

'Maybe when you've reached your target weight? I'm sure Biscuit would love to see you.'

Nora barked out a laugh. 'You're a trier, I'll give you that.' She became thoughtful for a moment. 'I hope you don't mind me asking, but when did your marriage break up?'

'Twelve years ago. You'd think I'd be over it by now.'

Her eyebrows rose. 'You're not?'

He poked his tongue into the side of his cheek as he considered his reply. 'Actually, I am. I don't love my ex anymore, if that's what you mean, but I don't seem to have moved on since I moved out. Or rather, was kicked out.'

'It wasn't amicable?'

'You could say that.' Elijah tried not to think about all the shouting, the crying, the recriminations, the accusations. There had been fault on both sides, his and hers, but she'd always laid the blame squarely on his shoulders.

'You've got a son, haven't you?'

'Yeah, Cameron. He's twenty-two.'

'It must have been hard on him.' She paused next to a low, flat outcrop of rock and lowered herself onto it.

Elijah sat next to her, Biscuit between them like a chaperone, and puffed out his cheeks. 'It was. Luckily, he follows me in that he loves his running – much to his mother's annoyance. It's the one thing we had in common, the one thing we could do together.'

'I see.' She didn't elaborate. She didn't need to, because he could tell by the sympathy on her face that she understood.

He hadn't been naïve enough to think that their running days would last forever, but he'd hoped they'd have lasted a while longer. 'You've not got any kids, have you?'

'Never met the right man to have them with, and didn't fancy giving motherhood a go on my own. Never been married either, and although I've had a couple of long-term relationships, nothing lasted. I had great fun on the way though, lived my best life.'

'You sound as though it's all over.'

She dropped her gaze. 'Nothing lasts forever, does it? Things change.'

He wanted to ask what, but with a note of finality she said, 'I don't know why I'm telling you all this,' and he guessed the subject was closed.

'Because you want me to feel sorry for you and withdraw my application to adopt this gorgeous chap?' he teased, putting his arm around the dog and pulling him close.

Biscuit gave him a slobbery wet lick on the chin, his expression happy. He clearly preferred it when the humans were discussing less weighty matters.

'Hey, you, get your hand off my dog!' she cried, and Biscuit licked her as well, making her giggle. It was a pretty sound, and one Elijah would like to hear more often.

With her arms around the dog, she looked happy and relaxed, and he found he couldn't take his eyes off her. He hadn't been kidding when he'd told her he thought she was perfect. Her face glowed and her hair shone in the afternoon sun, and when her lips parted in a smile, he wanted to kiss them.

What would she taste like, he wondered? Were her lips as soft as they looked? And would she close those lovely eyes and melt into him when he held her?

'What are you staring at?' she demanded, jerking him out of his thoughts and as he flailed around for an explanation, she asked, 'Have I got dog slobber on me?' She pointed to her face.

Relieved, he said, 'Just a smidge,' and wiped an imaginary streak off her cheek with his thumb. She was so close he could smell the warmth of the sun on her skin and the perfume she wore. His thumb tingled, and he closed his fist around it and looked away, fearing she might see the flare of desire in his eyes.

Biscuit made a soft sound in the back of his throat and wagged his tail, and Elijah was glad of the distraction the dog provided.

'It's lovely up here, isn't it?' Nora said.

Had she noticed his sudden discomfort, the awkwardness that he'd felt as the unfamiliar passion stirred him.

'It is,' he agreed, his voice sounding strange. He swallowed and put a hand up to his eyes to shade them as he stared absently at the view. He would have preferred to look at her, but he didn't dare.

Maybe it hadn't been a good idea to share such intimacies with her, to tell her things he usually kept private, but it was done now and he couldn't take them back. And he was still none the wiser about what made her eyes dim and her expression cloud, and why she'd cried on his shoulder.

Something was deeply troubling Nora and he wished he knew what it was, but he had a suspicion he'd never find out.

Maybe it was better he didn't, because he was thinking about her far more than was good for him, when she probably didn't think about him at all.

CHAPTER THIRTEEN

'I CRIED,' NORA TOLD Kendra with a wry, embarrassed twist of her lips. 'Sobbed like a baby.' She rolled her eyes at her own silliness. 'Elijah must think me a proper numpty.'

She'd just finished telling Kendra about her breakdown on the way to the kennels yesterday, as they set up for the day and before any customers arrived. It was Lori's day in college, so the pair of them were on their own.

'I'm sure he doesn't,' Kendra said. 'Anyway, from what I've heard, he isn't a bundle of laughs himself at the moment. I bumped into Christina on the way home yesterday, and she said he's been like a bear with a sore head lately.' The sideways look Kendra gave her, made Nora think that maybe *she* wasn't a bundle of laughs, either.

She was trying her best not to let it show (except for yesterday, when she'd fallen apart in spectacular fashion), but she had the feeling she wasn't succeeding. It was hard to get her head around the fact that she would never again be able to eat what she wanted, when she wanted. She would forever have to be careful about portion sizes and be mindful about how many carbs she consumed. It made her feel like a pariah, especially when friends and colleagues could walk into a cafe or restaurant and not worry what they ordered.

Nora hated to admit it, but she was scared that her life had changed forever. There would be no more partying, no more meals out, no more boozy nights in the pub with friends. And suddenly, without all that, she had no idea what to do with herself, or how she would occupy the long evenings on her own, even with Biscuit's help.

'I've lost another half a pound,' she announced brightly, hoping to lighten the gloom.

'That's brilliant. We should have a coffee and a cake to celebrate.'

That's what they always did when someone had good news to share. Or when the news was crap, for that matter, and one of them needed cheering up. A herbal tea and a lettuce leaf didn't have the same appeal, somehow, and Nora pulled a face.

Kendra winced. 'Sorry, wasn't thinking.'

'Don't let me stop you. Honestly, if you fancy a biscuit or a muffin, have one.'

'I don't like to. Not in front of you, when you can't.'

Nora rounded on her. 'Ken, this is *my* problem, not yours. I don't expect *you* to suffer because I've got to watch what I eat. I know you're being supportive, but it's not fair to you.'

'It's not fair to you, either.' Kendra laid a hand on her arm. 'Congrats on the half a pound, though,' she added.

Nora snorted and said, without thinking, 'Elijah told me he thinks I'm perfect as I am.' She'd thought, for one fleeting, ridiculous moment, that he'd been about to kiss her. Talk about letting her imagination run away with her. And what was really worrying was that she would have welcomed it, and she'd had to hug Biscuit tight to stop herself from throwing her arms around Elijah and snogging him senseless.

Kendra's eyes were out on stalks. 'He *did?*'

'Uh huh. I think he was just being nice.'

'I bet he wasn't. I think he fancies you.'

'Get off! He doesn't!' she scoffed, amused at the very idea of it. What would a fit, attractive man like Elijah, see in *her?* She was a wreck right now.

'You're blushing!'

'I am not. It's a hot flush.' Warmth was spreading up her chest and neck, and into her face.

Kendra grinned and nudged her with her hip as she went to unlock the door. 'I think you fancy him, too.'

'Do you want the sack? I can have your P45 ready for you by the end of the day,' Nora joked, but her heart wasn't in it because she knew Kendra was right. She *did* fancy him.

Kendra's smile grew wider. 'I don't blame you – he's a dish.'

'A dish?' Nora's tone was deadpan.

'The man's sexy, he's fit, and he can bake. What's not to like? If I was single, I'd be after him in a heartbeat.'

'The baking bit is of no interest to me,' Nora retorted.

'But the sexy and fit bits are, right?'

'Maybe; I'm not made of stone. But if you remember, *he's* the reason why I mightn't be able to adopt Biscuit.' Although she was still convinced that she was the more logical option to adopt the dog, nothing was certain. What if Elijah found some way of being able to take Biscuit to work with him? If that happened, her advantage would disappear.

Yes, she'd jump his bones in a heartbeat if the situation was different, but it was what it was. Nora hated that phrase, but it summed up the situation perfectly, and she really must stop thinking about Elijah that way, because no earthly good could possibly come of it.

ELIJAH WAS ALARMED when Andrea hurried into the bakery's kitchen, looking upset and flustered.

'I'm so sorry,' she began, 'I'm going to have to dash off. My dad's had a fall. I don't like leaving you in the lurch but—'

Elijah stopped her there. 'Just go, already. Don't worry about the bakery. Christina will be in soon and I'm sure we can manage without you for a couple of days, or however long you need to be off work.'

Andrea lifted her jacket from the hook and hoisted her bag onto her shoulder, her face suffused with anxiety.

'Let me know how he is, will you?' he asked. 'And tell me if there's anything I can do. *Anything,*' he repeated. He watched her dash out, worry pricking at him.

He hoped the news wasn't too bad. Andrea's father was in his eighties and quite frail, and she'd been trying to persuade him to move into Honeymead

Care Home in the village for some time, but the stubborn old so-and-so kept refusing to be swayed.

Elijah checked the timer on the oven, then washed his hands and stepped into the shop. Two customers were waiting patiently, and both expressed their concern as he served them.

He was in the middle of slicing and bagging a farmhouse loaf, when Kendra came in.

'Can you wait a sec?' he asked her, hearing the timer go off and sprinting into the kitchen. Cursing under his breath, he took the Bakewell tarts out of the oven and slid them onto a wire rack to cool, then hurried back to continue serving.

'On your own today?' she asked.

'Andrea had to dash off and Christina isn't in yet. What can I get you?'

'I'll have a choux bun and one of those, please.' Kendra pointed to a jambon (a square pastry filled with cheese and chunks of ham) which was a new recipe he'd decided to trial, even though his heart wasn't in it. It was good for business to have new products now and again, but he was finding it hard to summon the enthusiasm he'd once had for his craft.

He popped her purchases in a bag and as he was handing over her change, he asked, 'Could you give this to Nora?' He held out a paper bag. 'I've been trying some new bakes, and I thought she might like a taste. It's only a morsel of each, because... you know.' He didn't like to mention anything about her being on a diet, in case he came across as judgemental or unsupportive. In his experience, it was never a good idea to comment on a woman's weight, or what she was, or wasn't, eating. His ex had been forever on a diet.

Kendra peeped into the bag. 'These look yummy, but please don't be offended if she doesn't eat them. Since her diagnosis, she's been so good – apart from that blip on Saturday evening. I don't think I'd have her willpower or determination, if I had diabetes.'

Elijah froze. 'She's got *diabetes?*'

'Yes, she—' Kendra stopped, let out a gasp and clapped a hand to her mouth. Her eyes widened, then she closed them briefly. When she opened them again, he saw the dismay on her face. 'You didn't know, did you?'

He shook his head.

'Aw, hell. Nora is going to kill me. I assumed you knew. Bugger.'

'I won't say anything,' he assured her.

'I'll have to tell her I let slip. Can you not say anything though, until I've had a chance to confess? I'll try to catch her before she leaves to see Biscuit, but the salon is busy ,and I don't want to tell her when there are clients around in case she gets cross.'

'Is that likely?'

'Ordinarily I'd say no, but these past few weeks, since she was diagnosed, she hasn't been herself.'

She only found out a few weeks ago? Elijah was shocked. No wonder she'd burst into tears yesterday. And no wonder she wanted to lose weight. He used to know a runner who was diabetic – although in remission now – and the guy used to swear that maintaining a healthy weight, keeping his carbohydrate intake low, and doing loads of exercise was what helped him stay well and avoid the complications that the disease could all too often cause.

Deep in thought, he didn't notice Kendra leave.

NORA WAS LOOKING forward to seeing Biscuit today (of course she was!), but she was apprehensive about seeing Elijah. If he was kind to her again, she might throw herself at him, and that would never do.

She'd just changed out of the black trousers she wore for work and into a pair of leggings, and was doing up the laces on her trainers, when Kendra cornered her.

'Can I have a word?'

'If it's quick,' Nora said, but something in the tone of Kendra's voice made her stop and look up.

Kendra was chewing on her lip. 'I've got something to tell you. I'm sorry, but I let the cat out of the bag with Elijah.'

'What cat?'

'I let slip you're diabetic. Sorry, Nora, but I assumed he knew.'

Nora sat up and sighed, resigned. She supposed it was inevitable people would find out eventually. She'd hoped that telling everyone she was on a diet because she wanted to lose weight, would be enough to stop any speculation, but when she'd reached her target weight and was still avoiding carbs like the plague, she had to expect that questions would be asked and assumptions made. All she'd wanted was an opportunity to come to terms with it herself, before she shared her news with all and sundry. Anyway, from what she'd learnt online, diabetes was far more common than she'd initially realised, and growing more common by the year, so she didn't feel quite as alone, despite not personally knowing anyone with the condition.

'It's okay,' she assured her. 'I would have told him myself before long.' She wouldn't have, but Kendra didn't need to know that. It would only make her feel bad. Nora got to her feet. 'I'd better be off.' She smiled ruefully. 'And I'll try my best not to bawl my eyes out today.'

'It's bound to be hard, and you're doing so well. I admire your fortitude. You haven't even had a nibble of those little cakes Elijah gave you.'

'I daren't. I wouldn't have stopped at a nibble. See you tomorrow. Any issues, give me a ring,' she said. 'Fingers crossed I won't have to do this for much longer.'

The sanctuary's manager should be back from her holidays next week, and hopefully she'd make a decision one way or the other.

When Nora arrived at The Forever Home, she waved to Jakob as she made her way towards Biscuit's kennel. Almost as though the dog could tell time, he was waiting at the door, his tail waving, and when he saw her, he woofed gently.

A lead and a harness were hanging on a hook ready, and she lifted them off, opened the door and slipped inside. Biscuit nudged her, pressing his cold wet nose into her palm, and she knelt to hug him.

Putting her arms around him, Nora buried her face in his fluffy neck.

'Want to go for a walk?'

He wagged his tail, but it was followed by a whine, and when she got to her feet, she noticed him staring through the bars. He whined again, and a pang struck Nora in the chest when she realised that Biscuit was hoping to see Elijah. So was she.

He was late, which wasn't like him. Should she wait?

She'd give it five minutes, she decided.

When the five minutes became ten and he still hadn't showed, she said, 'I don't think Elijah's coming today. It looks like it's just you and me, poppet.'

Biscuit glanced up at her with puppy dog eyes, his ears down, his expression sad, and Nora felt dreadful. Did he prefer Elijah to her? Had she lost the war for his affection?

'Everything okay, Nora?' Maisie asked. She had a bucket in one hand and a stiff-bristled broom in the other.

'I'm not sure. Elijah hasn't turned up, and Biscuit seems to be missing him.'

'He probably is. You and Elijah have always visited him as a couple, so he's wondering where he is today.'

Nora feared there was more to it than that. She worried that Biscuit had bonded more with Elijah than with her.

And when she took him out for his walk, the feeling was reinforced by his reluctance to go far. The dog kept stopping and looking back over his shoulder, as though he expected Elijah to appear at any second. It was only when they'd left the kennels behind and were on the open moorland, did he begin to relax and accept that it was going to be just the two of them.

Nora was surprised to discover how nervous she was walking Biscuit on her own. He was a big dog, well-built and powerful, and if he decided he wanted to go somewhere, Nora had a feeling that was the direction they'd go in.

However, Biscuit was as well behaved as usual, plodding sedately by her side, only occasionally yanking her back when he stopped suddenly to sniff an interesting smell. When that happened, she had no choice but to stop too, until he'd sniffed his fill.

The moorland was dotted with sheep, the occasional cow or two, a few stunted trees, and several clumps of large rocks. Nora picked one at random and sat on it,

Biscuit jumping up next to her, cuddling in, and when he nuzzled her ear then licked her on the cheek, her insides turned to mush.

Now that her initial nervousness at being able to handle Biscuit had faded, Nora felt incredibly safe with him by her side.

There was something missing, though: *Elijah*. This walk simply wasn't the same without him.

CHAPTER FOURTEEN

ELIJAH SURVEYED THE selection of sweet (ish) treats on the counter critically. They looked good enough to eat – but *were* they? He'd sampled so many, that he was now taste-blind, yet there were so many more he wanted to bake.

He was also exhausted, since it was gone nine p.m. and he'd been on his feet all day. As soon as the shop had closed at its customary four o'clock, Elijah had popped into the salon and had a quick word with Kendra to check that Nora was okay, then he'd begun work on a whole new range of recipes, most of which he hadn't had the necessary ingredients for, so he'd had to drive to the supermarket in Thornbury, and even they'd lacked a couple of items, so he'd had to do a mad dash to the health food shop in the precinct as well. Then he'd set to, hoping he'd remembered everything.

Three and a half hours later, he had baked brownies, flapjacks, chocolate chip cookies, peanut butter bombs, and he'd even made fudge. All of them with as little carbs and sugar as possible. Now all he had to do was to get someone to taste them and give him their verdict.

And he knew just the person.

The question he was currently asking himself was whether it was too late to go knocking on Nora's door?

Possibly, but he didn't want to wait. He was too wound up to leave it until tomorrow, and there was also the added problem that she mightn't appreciate what he'd done. If that was the case, he'd prefer to have his efforts thrown back in his face in private, and not in the middle of the salon.

Making a decision, he boxed up a few of each and had just put the last of the selection into the box when his phone rang.

It was Andrea. He'd been hoping she'd call with an update on her dad. He'd sent her a text to say he was thinking of her, but hadn't heard a peep from her until now.

'How's your dad?' he asked immediately.

She sounded tired as she replied, 'Not good. He's fractured his hip, which I kind of suspected, and he needs an operation. I expect he'll be in hospital for a while. In the meantime, I'll try to get him a place in

Honeymead, so when he is discharged, he can go there. Whether that'll be permanent, I don't know. What I do know, is that he'll not be able to manage on his own for a long time – if ever. I suppose we'll have to see how it goes.'

'I'm so sorry, Andrea. As I said, if there's anything I can do, anything you need...'

'I hate to do this to you, but I'm going to need a fair bit of time off.'

'No problem; I assumed that would be the case.' How to staff the shop had been playing on his mind ever since she'd left earlier. He didn't want to take anyone else on, but he might have to, even if it was temporary.

He'd think about that later, though.

For once, Elijah didn't clean up after himself. Although the kitchen wasn't in too bad a shape considering the action it had seen this evening, it wasn't up to his usual exacting standard. Anything less than spotless was unacceptable, but this evening he was eager to get away. He'd simply have to rise extra early tomorrow morning to give the place a good scrub before baking the first of the day's loaves. He didn't mind. What he was about to do now, was far more important than grabbing a bit more sleep.

All he hoped was that Nora approved these new bakes, and he wasn't about to make a complete fool of himself.

WHEN NORA'S DOORBELL rang, she automatically checked the time. It was ten past nine, a bit late in the evening for uninvited guests, especially on a Monday, so before she answered it she peered through the spyhole. Then stepped back with a gasp when she saw Elijah standing there.

What did *he* want?

There was only one way to find out, so she opened the door. 'Where were you today? Biscuit missed you.' Damn, should she have told him that? It was better than what she'd almost said though, which was that *she'd* missed him.

'Andrea wasn't in. Um, I hope you don't mind, but I've brought you these.' He held up a familiar-looking box.

Nora couldn't begin to count the number of times she'd carried one of those white cardboard boxes from the bakery to the salon, careful not to jostle its sweet and usually gooey contents.

She glowered at him. 'Is this your idea of a joke?'

'No, of course not!' He looked flustered now, the light from the hallway illuminating the sudden flush of colour on his cheeks.

'I know you know, because Kendra told me.'

'That's why I'm here. I've been working on a batch of new recipes, and I thought you might like to try them.'

Nora snorted. 'Dear lord, don't you *know* that diabetics shouldn't eat sweet stuff? And I'm trying to cut out carbs, too – and that means flour, in case you hadn't realised. So no, I *don't* want to try them. Sheesh!'

He held out the box to her. 'The recipes I've been working on *are* suitable for diabetics – I hope. Can I come in? Please?'

'You hope,' she echoed flatly. 'That's not much help.' She moved aside anyway and jerked her head. 'Five minutes.'

When he sidled past her in the narrow hall, she smelt that familiar tantalising aroma of sugar and syrup which seemed to ooze out of his pores, and she ground her teeth together as the urge to kiss him swept through her. Would he taste as sweet as he smelled, she mused, not for the first time. She wouldn't be surprised if he did, and wouldn't that do wonders for her self-control? *Not.* At the first taste, she'd want to gobble him up whole; either that, or devour every single thing in that box of his and beg for more.

He hovered in the hall by the door to the living room and she flapped a hand, urging him to go ahead of her, and kept flapping until he was safely inside so she didn't have to squeeze past him again.

'Well?' she demanded, her hands on her ample hips. It struck her that she must look a mess in her fluffy pink pyjamas with equally fluffy pink slipper socks on her feet. And she dreaded to think what her hair was doing or how her face looked without any make-up.

She shouldn't have answered the door. But it was too late now.

Elijah shuffled over to the dining room table that she rarely used, preferring to eat off a tray on her lap in front of the telly, and placed the box down gently. When he opened the lid, she caught another waft of forbidden deliciousness.

'Hear me out,' he began, before she had a chance to speak. 'I've been doing some research, and I hope I've found some treats you *can* eat.'

Okay, now she was intrigued. 'What sort of treats?'

'After Kendra let slip that you've recently been diagnosed with diabetes – I'm sorry about that, by the way.'

'My diagnosis, or that Kendra told you?'

'Your diagnosis – although I hope you didn't give Kendra a hard time, because it was an honest mistake.'

Nora wanted to growl at him, but she settled for a sharp, 'I did not give Kendra a hard time.'

He smiled. She didn't return it, and it soon subsided. 'That's a relief. I'd hate to think I was the cause of any trouble between you.'

'Don't flatter yourself.'

'Anyway, I found a recipe for brownies that some famous doctor on the telly recommended, so I thought I'd give it a go since it's supposed to be for people who want to control their blood glucose and also to lose weight – as part of a calorie-controlled diet, obviously. I wouldn't recommend eating six of them in one go. One would be enough.'

'Where's the fun in that?'

His expression told her that he wasn't sure whether she was joking or not.

She wasn't.

'Do you want to know what's in them?' He picked up a small brown square and held it up.

'Go on then, astound me.'

Elijah took a breath. 'Almond flour – not wheat flour – coconut oil, eggs, dates, cacao nibs and cacao powder, plus a few other ingredients such as baking powder and salt.' He held up a hand as she was about to speak. 'The almond flour does contain carbs, but nowhere near the amount that normal flour has, and the cacao nibs are tiny, crushed pieces of cacao beans which is the purest form of chocolate. Apparently they're a good source of antioxidants and contain loads of fibre. As do the dates, which also give the brownies their sweetness – but don't worry, dates are good for you,' he added hurriedly. 'Lots of fibre.'

Nora wrinkled her nose, unconvinced. It did look utterly yummy, but how could she trust that it wouldn't send her blood glucose level rocketing? Her GP had been adamant that she had to be very careful about what she put in her mouth, and she was fairly certain that brownies were on the naughty list.

'I've checked the number of calories in each piece, as well as the carb content, fibre and protein,' Elijah told her.

'How did you do that?'

'There's an app you can download that'll count the calories for you.'

That was news to Nora. Mind you, she'd never counted calories in her life, so it wasn't surprising she hadn't heard of it. 'Show me.'

He already had his mobile in his hand. He passed it to her and she studied it in amazement.

'Do you mind if I...?' she asked.

'Go ahead.'

As she worked her way around the app, she was amazed. Gosh, this would be a game-changer. Yes, she'd still have to weigh and measure every sip and crumb that passed her lips (except for water), but she'd be able to see precisely the number of calories she was consuming, and all the sneaky carbs and sugar hidden in loads of different foods.

'Wow...' Despite herself, a smile spread across her face. Even if Elijah had brought forbidden food into her house, she would forgive him a hundred times because of this.

When she handed his phone back to him, she'd already decided to download the app, no matter the cost. Even if she had to live on leaves for the next month to afford it. Oh, wait a sec, leaves were *exactly* what she was living on!

'Would you like to try a bite?' Elijah broke off a morsel of brownie.

Nora snatched it out of his hand and stuffed it in her mouth. The burst of nutty chocolate sweetness made her groan in delight. 'This is so good,' she mumbled.

His face broke into a wide grin.

'Can I have the rest of it?'

'Don't you want to try any of the others?'

Of course she did. And when he explained that the chocolate chip cookies were made with a small amount of eighty-five per cent dark chocolate and a nominal amount of artificial sweetener, and that the fudge was made with a decent portion of cream cheese, she was sold.

By the end of the tasting session, she was elated. 'I can still have a treat now and again,' she said, tears in her eyes. 'Thank you *so* much.'

'My pleasure. I mean it. I've had the best time this evening making these.'

'Have you found your baking mojo again?'

'I think I have.'

She beamed at him, and he beamed back. And suddenly she was in his arms and tasting *him* – and she wasn't surprised to discover he tasted even better than anything that had come out of the little white box.

Nora's eyes drifted shut as she lost herself in his embrace. His tongue found hers and her pulse pounded in her ears, her heart hammering so loudly that it drowned out the voice in her head advising caution as she lost herself to the kiss.

Elijah was the first to draw back. He was breathing hard and his eyes glittered. He dropped his gaze. 'I didn't mean for that to happen.'

'Neither did I.'

'I don't want you to think—'

'Don't worry, I don't,' she interjected. To stop the tremble in her legs, she leant against the table and wrapped her arms around herself.

He swallowed, and she noticed that his jaw was tense as he rubbed a hand across his chin. She wanted to take that hand and put it on her breast. She wanted to kiss his neck, to run her fingers up underneath his tee shirt. She wanted to take him to bed and make love to him.

She did none of those things. 'Thanks again for the cookies,' she said, her voice stilted and formal.

'You're welcome.' He sounded cold, a shock of chilled water dousing the heat of her desire. It was a clear rejection.

'See you tomorrow at the kennels,' she said. She needed him out of her house *now,* before she did something she'd regret.

Elijah gave her a long, steady stare. 'No, I don't think you will,' he said.

Then he was gone, leaving her to spend the rest of the night and long into the morning wondering what he meant – when she wasn't reliving the feel of his lips on hers.

CHAPTER FIFTEEN

TO SAY THAT NORA was in shock was an understatement, but when she woke the following morning, her thoughts immediately went to Elijah, and she pressed a finger to her lips. Had she really kissed him?

It wasn't the kiss that floored her – it was how she'd felt when it happened. She'd enjoyed it, but it was more than that. It had felt right in a way that no other kiss ever had. It had been new and exciting, yet familiar and comforting, as though she had slipped into a warm, soft bed.

But there had been nothing soft about Elijah, her wicked mind pointed out. He'd been very happy about the kiss. *Very* happy indeed.

Reining in her naughty thoughts, she wondered why he'd ended it if he'd been as into it as he'd appeared to be. Even though it probably wouldn't have been a good idea and would have complicated matters enormously when it came to Biscuit, she would have loved to have seen where it might have led (yeah, as if she didn't know!) but he'd pulled away and told her he hadn't meant for it to happen. Then he'd got all weird and stilted on her.

When she arrived at the salon, Nora decided to keep the kiss to herself; however, she did tell Kendra about Elijah's surprise visit with the diabetic-friendly cakes.

'Ooh, that's so romantic!' Kendra cried.

'Shh, keep your voice down.' Nora peered around the door of the back room, making sure Lori hadn't heard. The salon wouldn't open for another five minutes, and they were busy making coffee (black for Nora – yuck), while Lori was fluffing and folding the towels and putting them on the shelf near the basins.

Whispering now, Kendra said, 'See, I *told* you he fancied you.'

'He saw a business opportunity and decided to give it a whirl.' *Forget the kiss, forget the kiss...*

Kendra gave her a measured look and raised her eyebrows. 'If that's all there was to it, he wouldn't have turned up at nine o'clock in the evening. He'd have waited until today. What were the cakes like? Were they any good?'

'I've brought some in for you to try. I only had a nibble of each, but they tasted mighty fine to me. Mind you, these days an apple tastes pretty good, so I think my tastebuds are knackered. See what you think.' She took the box out of her bag and put it on the countertop.

Kendra peered inside. 'They look lovely. What are they?'

'That one's a brownie, that's a chocolate chip cookie, that's a peanut butter bomb thing.' Nora thought she'd shown exceptional self-control by only having a small mouthful of each, considering that after Elijah had left she'd felt like stuffing the lot in her face in one go.

Instead, she'd had a large glass of ice-cold water, hoping it would stifle her greed and douse the flames of her lust at the same time. Though, to be fair, he'd done a pretty good job of dousing those himself, when he'd gone all cold and formal on her.

'Lori, I've got some goodies if you want to grab one before Kendra eats them all,' Nora called, and Lori came hurrying in.

'Fudge! Yum.' The girl took a piece. 'Does this mean you're off the diet?'

'Not at all. A... friend...' She hesitated over what to call him '...made them. They're... um...' She caught Kendra's eye, who nodded. 'Suitable for diabetics.'

Lori stared at her. 'Is that supposed to mean something?'

'It means I'm diabetic.'

'Okay.' Lori shrugged.

Nora blinked, taken aback. She'd expected... To be honest, she hadn't known *what* to expect. To be judged, maybe? To be pitied?

Lori did neither. She merely dipped her hand back in the box and brought out another treat. 'Mmm, these are *so* good.'

'They are, aren't they?' Nora replied, and smiled when Kendra gave her arm a reassuring rub. Suddenly, life – diet-wise, at least – was looking up.

Now all she had to do was become Biscuit's new owner and control her growing feelings for Elijah.

Easy-peasy!

AS NORA HURRIED past the bakery on her way to the kennels, she noticed Andrea wasn't in her customary position behind the counter, and she wondered whether that might be the reason for Elijah's cryptic comment about not seeing her at the kennels today. He was having to man the shop again.

'Her dad's had a fall,' Christina said when Nora asked after her. 'So she won't be in for a while. I can get a message to her if you want?'

'Gosh, no. It wasn't anything important. Tell her I'm thinking of her, if you speak to her.'

She considered asking to have a quick word with Elijah, but the place was busy and Christina looked a little frazzled, so she thought she'd better leave it.

As Nora made her way up Muddypuddle Lane, her emotions were conflicted. If Elijah had been able to visit the kennels this afternoon, how would it have been between them? Awkward, perhaps? Would he have wanted to talk about last night, or would he have brushed it under the carpet and tried to pretend it hadn't happened?

'What do you think, Biscuit?' she asked the dog, as she led him across the moor on what was quickly becoming her favourite walk. 'Do you think Elijah is regretting kissing me?'

Biscuit booped her leg with his nose and gazed up at her with soulful eyes.

'No, I don't know, either. I wish I did, because I really like him.'

Biscuit woofed softly.

'You do too, don't you, boy. Are you going to miss him when you come to live with me?'

Another woof.

Nora eyed him speculatively. She was becoming more and more convinced the dog could understand her. 'If you had to choose between us, which one would you pick, I wonder?'

Biscuit stopped to sniff at a clump of grass, then sat down and stared at her.

She wasn't entirely sure what this meant. Was he trying to tell her that he preferred her? Or Elijah? Or that he couldn't choose?

Thankfully, he wouldn't have to – that decision would be down to Dawn, the centre's manager, who would be back in less than a week. Which was something Nora was incredibly nervous about.

Biscuit got to his feet, but it was Nora's turn to stop as a thought occurred to her. *Andrea.* How was Elijah going to manage if she was off work for any length of time? Abruptly Nora despised herself for thinking that Andrea's misfortune might give her an advantage in the Biscuit adoption stakes.

'Nora Bunting,' she said out loud, 'you're turning into a horrid person.' Which kind of spoilt the rest of what should have been a very pleasant walk with her furry friend.

Her mood hadn't improved by the time she put Biscuit back in his kennel, and as she sank to her knees to give him one last cuddle, she felt quite depressed. Even the prospect of being able to have the occasional yummy cookie or brownie didn't cheer her up.

But then Jakob told her something that *should* have cheered her, but in fact had the opposite effect: it made her feel worse.

'Nora, I've got good news,' he said. 'Elijah has withdrawn his application for Biscuit.'

'AFTER WHAT YOU'VE just told me, how can you say Elijah doesn't have the hots for you?' Kendra demanded when Nora popped into the salon later to check that the afternoon had gone smoothly. She'd also wanted to share her news.

'He doesn't,' Nora insisted. 'He knows I'm the better option, because without Andrea he's a bit stuck, and Christina thinks she's going to be off for a while so he's going to have to spend more time in the shop, which wouldn't be fair on Biscuit.'

'So why do you look so miserable?'

'I feel sorry for him, I suppose.'

'That's not all you feel,' Kendra suggested, and as Nora glowered at her, she pressed on, 'How long have we known each other? A bloody long time, that's how long,' she said, before Nora could respond. 'And I've never seen you this het up over a bloke.'

'I'm not het up over a bloke.' She *was*, but she wasn't going to admit it. 'I'm het up over a *dog*.'

'Even though you've no longer got any reason to be?'

'What can I say? It takes me a while to adjust.'

'Pah!' Kendra scoffed. 'Your middle name is spontaneity.'

'Not anymore.'

'It's really knocked you for six, hasn't it, this diabetes?'

Nora shrugged, trying to be nonchalant but not fooling anyone, least of all herself.

And there was another thing she couldn't fool herself about, and that was her acute disappointment that with Elijah throwing in the towel, she had no reason to see him again.

'**THIS IS NICE.**' Elijah's gaze swept around the restaurant, then returned to his son.

Cameron was studying the menu. 'Hmm?'

'I said, this is nice. The two of us, out for dinner.'

'Yeah, it is. What are you having?'

Elijah hadn't looked at his menu yet. 'Not sure.'

'Steak for me, I think, with loads of chips. Protein for muscle, carbs for energy. I'll have a side of garlic bread, as well. I'm carb-loading for tomorrow.'

'What's happening tomorrow?'

Cameron stared at him disbelievingly. 'The last training session before the British RunMad Fifty Miler.'

'That's *this* Saturday?'

'Duh, yeah. Don't tell me you forgot? You always run it.'

'Not this year.' Elijah had entered but wouldn't be taking part. It would be the first one he'd miss since the event began, eleven years ago. Every country held its own RunMad fifty-mile endurance race, usually on the same weekend simultaneously, and he'd seen the event go from strength to strength. But even if he hadn't put his running shoes out to pasture, he wouldn't have been able to take part this year. With his leg having been in a boot for so long, he wouldn't have been fit enough. However, he'd have looked on in envy from the sidelines, and would have given loads of virtual pats on the back.

Elijah suddenly felt very cut off from everything he held dear. Even his own son.

Cameron closed the menu. 'Sorry, Dad, I keep forgetting.'

That's what Elijah had been trying to do: forget that he'd once ran ultra marathons, forget that he'd once ran at all. And he'd almost managed it until the new life he'd begun to forge had fallen apart.

As though Cameron could read his mind, he asked, 'What's happening on the dog front? Cookie, isn't it?'

'Biscuit,' Elijah reminded him. 'Nothing. I've withdrawn my application.'

'Why? I thought you'd fallen in love with him. Don't tell me you're letting that woman have him?'

'Her need is greater than mine.' He'd mentioned to Cameron when he'd first seen Biscuit that someone else was interested in the dog, but he hadn't said a lot since.

Cameron's gaze bore into him. 'That's very noble of you. But from where I'm sitting, I think you've got a need, too.'

'I've been baking.'

'What are you on about?' Cameron frowned. 'You're a *baker*, you bake for a *living,* so of course you're baking. Or is there something you're not telling me?' His concern was obvious.

'I know I bake every day, but this is different. I'm enjoying it again.'

'Hold on, I'm confused. One minute we're talking about the dog, and the next we're talking about baking. What's the connection? Have you given up on the dog *because* you're enjoying baking? Is that it?'

The two weren't connected and Elijah hesitated, wondering how to explain when he wasn't sure he understood it himself.

All he knew was that Nora needed Biscuit more than he did. But, hell, he was going to miss the goofball, and he was going to miss Nora, too. More than he thought possible.

He blamed it on the kiss. But he knew it was more than that – he'd fallen for her.

He wasn't going to share that little nugget with Cameron, though. Not once since the divorce had Elijah mentioned another woman to his son, and he wasn't about to start now, especially since there wasn't anything *to* mention. It wasn't as though he and Nora were dating, was it?

However, Cameron was more perceptive than Elijah gave him credit for. 'Is it because of this woman?' he asked.

'She's called Nora.'

'Why is her need greater than yours?'

'Her life has been turned upside down, I suppose.'

'So has yours.'

'Yes, but...'

'What's she like?'

Gorgeous, he wanted to say but didn't. Something in his face or the way he hesitated must have given him away though, because Cameron asked, 'Is there anything going on between you?'

'No.' Elijah was adamant about that.

'Would you like there to be?'

Elijah didn't reply.

'What's stopping you, Dad? Is she married or in a relationship?'

'No.'

'What, then?'

'She isn't interested.'

'How do you know? Have you asked her?'

'Of course not!' The very thought horrified him.

'I didn't think so. How do you know she isn't interested, then?'

'I just know.'

'Don't take this the wrong way, Dad, but you're not the best judge when it comes to women and their feelings.'

'Did your mum say that?'

'She didn't have to.'

'I really ballsed it up with her, didn't I?'

'Don't beat yourself up. The two of you weren't compatible, that's all. Shit happens.' Cameron reached out and touched his hand in a rare gesture of affection. 'I just want you to be happy, Dad.'

'Since when did you sound so grown up?'

'I *am* grown up.'

'Yeah, you are.' Elijah gazed at his son as though seeing him for the first time. Where had the years gone? It seemed only yesterday he was holding a squalling pink faced scrap in his arms. 'I'm so proud of you,' he said, his voice thick with emotion.

'I'm proud of you too, Dad.' Then the atmosphere lightened, and the moment faded as Cameron said, 'Can we order now? I'm starving.'

But though the conversation moved onto less serious matters, Elijah couldn't stop thinking about it. It had been many years since he'd been happy. What a waste.

CHAPTER SIXTEEN

NORA FILLED THE metal bowl with fresh water and put it down on the plastic easy-wipe mat next to the fridge.

'There you go,' she told Biscuit, and he wagged his tail but made no move to drink from it. This was his first day in his new home, and he seemed rather uncertain about the whole thing.

'You'll get used to it,' she promised, stroking the top of his head and praying that was the case. He'd been padding around ever since she'd fetched him from the kennels nearly two hours ago, and was showing no signs of settling in.

Nora had shown him the garden, his nice new dog bed (with a blanket brought from The Forever Home at Jakob's suggestion), and the cupboard where his food and toys were kept. She'd offered to groom him (he'd sidled away), and play with him (he hadn't shown any interest, not even in the ball with the squeaker), and she'd tried to get him to cuddle on the sofa but he was having none of it.

Biscuit was too busy exploring every nook and cranny. Which Nora wouldn't have minded, but he'd already explored each one several times already. He reminded her of a wild animal in a cage, pacing back and forth.

Maybe she should take him for a walk? Would a spot of exercise help? It couldn't hurt, she decided, lifting his lead off the rack of coat hooks by the back door. 'Walkies?'

His ears pricked up and a hopeful expression lit up his soft brown eyes.

She'd take him for a stroll around the village and pay the salon a visit while she was at it, because it would be a good idea to introduce him to the place and to her staff, since he'd be coming into work with her tomorrow. She hoped Kendra and the others would like him...

Feeling anxious (Biscuit was probably picking up on her anxiety) Nora popped his harness on him and set out. She'd taken today off in order to collect him from The Forever Home (having been given the green light by Dawn yesterday, who had been lovely when she'd done her home visit) and help him settle in. Nora knew it might take a few days – and Jakob had told her the same – but she was nevertheless concerned. She desperately wanted Biscuit to be happy in his new home.

Thankfully he seemed much more relaxed now he was outside, content to stop and sniff at all the unfamiliar smells. The high street had a typical Wednesday lunchtime busyness about it. Picklewick wasn't a big place, but enough people lived and worked there to keep businesses like the cafe, her salon, and the bakery afloat, and most of the faces she met were familiar. If she hadn't cut their hair and therefore knew them personally, she knew them by name or by sight, so it was to be expected that several people would stop to chat. And to admire Biscuit, of course.

Biscuit, to Nora's relief, lapped up the attention. He was definitely a people dog, friendly and calm.

Until he suddenly wasn't...

Nora hadn't been expecting the dog to take off down the pavement at a rate of knots, and she was almost yanked off her feet. With an excited woof, he barrelled into the road, dragging her with him, and was met with a squeal of brakes and honking horns.

Nora had no idea how either of them arrived at the other side of the street in one piece. It was a wonder they hadn't been killed, or at the very least, injured.

Stumbling over the kerb, she almost face-planted the pavement.

'What the hell are you playing at?' an all-too familiar voice demanded, and Nora looked up to see Elijah's angry and shocked blue eyes boring into hers.

Stunned, she stuttered, 'I didn't mean... He caught me...'

Elijah ignored her. Crouching down, he put his palms on either side of the dog's head. 'Are you okay, boy?'

Biscuit was fine. He was gazing lovingly at Elijah, his tail wagging nineteen to the dozen.

It was *Nora* who wasn't fine.

She was trembling, her knees felt weak, her heart was pounding so hard she feared she might pass out, and she was trying her best not to cry.

'He could have been run over,' Elijah scolded.

Anger surged through her, boiling away the threatened tears. 'So could I,' she shot back.

'You should have had better control of him.'

'I didn't expect him to dart across the bloody road.'

'Maybe you should have?'

A scathing retort leapt into her mind. And there it stayed. Elijah was right. She *should* have been more prepared. It didn't have to be Elijah who caught Biscuit's attention next time; it could be another dog, or a cat, or a squirrel that he wanted to say hello to or chase.

Oh, hell, had she bitten off more than she could chew? Had she made the wrong decision? Although Biscuit had pulled on his lead before, he'd always responded to a firm 'no' and the pulling had stopped.

This, however, hadn't been a pull. It had been a full-on, totally unexpected *lunge*. And Nora hadn't had a hope in hell of holding him back.

Telling herself she'd be better prepared from now on, she tugged on the lead to get Biscuit's attention, and Elijah got to his feet.

'Thank you for your concern,' she said icily. 'It won't happen again.'

'I hope not. You could have—'

She snarled, 'Yes, thank you! I'm well aware of what *could* have happened since *I'm* the one it nearly happened to. Good day to you.' And with that she stalked off, shaken, but trying to muster her dignity.

And had she *really* said, 'Good day to you,' like some elderly spinster from a nineteenth century BBC drama?

Without going to the salon and having lost her appetite for a walk, Nora slunk back home, her tail between her legs. To add insult to (almost) injury, Biscuit's tail was waving like a flag in a stiff north-easterly, and he looked the happiest she'd seen him since she'd brought him home.

ELIJAH FELT AWFUL. He shouldn't have reacted the way he had, but he'd nearly had a heart attack when he'd seen Biscuit drag Nora into the road. Admittedly, the traffic had been slow, but that was beside the point. She could have been killed. They both could.

Having a go at her had been his way of dealing with the sudden fear and his subsequent relief. Adrenalin had flooded his body, making his legs feel weak and his heart race. He'd also felt sick and shaken, but he shouldn't have taken it out on her.

Then again, he was right in saying she should have had better control over the dog. Biscuit might look cute and fluffy, and he was incredibly gentle, but he didn't know his own strength, and when he'd spied Elijah on the opposite pavement, he'd made a beeline for him.

Elijah stomped off home with mixed feelings. He was delighted to have seen Biscuit, but not under those circumstances. He was also delighted to have seen Nora, but ditto to the circumstances. Despite her shocked and rather hostile demeanour, she'd looked gorgeous. Having not seen her for over a week (nine days, to be exact – not that he was counting), Elijah had drunk her in.

She'd lost a couple of pounds, he thought. That should please her. And she'd had her hair cut. Not by much, but enough to notice. Enough for *him* to notice, because he'd committed the smallest details to memory. Like the dimple in her left cheek when she smiled, and her slightly wonky front tooth, and the way the short fine hairs curled at the base of her neck.

He should apologise. It was only right. He'd take her some cake; he'd been trialling another new recipe and—

On second thoughts, best not. He didn't want her to think he only wanted her for her taste-testing ability.

Flowers! That was it.

Elijah executed a smart about-turn and hurried back to the high street. He would buy a nice bouquet and deliver it personally. And if she was still out on her walk, he'd wait until she got back, because, let's face it, he didn't have much else to do this afternoon as Andrea was at the bakery today. She was managing to do a couple of days a week but wasn't back full time yet and wouldn't be for a while.

Her dad was on the mend though, so that was the main thing, and what was even better news was that the old chap had agreed to take a look at Honeymead when he was discharged from the hospital.

Elijah hadn't bought flowers for at least a decade, so when he entered the florist's shop and came face to face with buckets of blooms, he had no idea what to go for.

'Need any help?' the woman behind the counter asked.

'I'm after some flowers.'

To her credit, she didn't roll her eyes. 'Then you've come to the right place. Any idea what you'd like?'

'No?'

'What's the occasion? Birthday, anniversary...?'

'An apology.'

'Ah.' She nodded her understanding. 'Who is it for? Wife, girlfriend, mum?'

The words were out of Elijah's mouth before his brain could rein them in. 'For someone I *wish* was my girlfriend.'

'I see. Do you want it delivered?'

'Can I take it with me?'

'Of course. Give me a few minutes and I'll put something together, and you can let me know what you think.'

Elijah watched her select several flowers and stems of foliage, holding them in her hand as she fitted them together, turning the growing bouquet this way and that until she was happy with the result.

'I think Nora will like them,' she said, startling him.

 '*Nora?*' How did she know?

'I take it these *are* for her?'

'You saw.' *Of course* the woman had seen, he realised in dismay. She would have had a front-row seat from her a shop window.

'I did.'

'I wasn't very nice.' He hung his head in shame.

'You saw someone you care about almost get flattened by an SUV. No wonder you were upset. It's like when I lost my five-year-old in the supermarket once. When I found him, I shouted at him, too. Then I cried.'

'At least I didn't cry,' he replied wryly. But he'd felt like it.

'Here you go.' She handed him the prettily wrapped bouquet. 'Good luck.'

Elijah suspected he was going to need more than luck, because he didn't just care about Nora, he was totally and utterly in love with her.

In that split second when he'd seen her being dragged into the path of an oncoming car, his heart had almost stopped. He'd lunged forward, and time had splintered and slowed as fear swept through him. Every instinct had screamed at him that he needed to reach her, to throw himself between her and the hunk of metal bearing down on her, but he'd not been quick enough, as Biscuit's momentum had thankfully pulled her clear and she'd stumbled onto the pavement.

His relief on seeing her safe, had turned to anger. How could she have been so stupid to let Biscuit drag her across the road like that! The thought of what could have happened made him feel sick. A world without Nora in it, was unthinkable.

He had no idea how he'd managed to fall for someone so quickly or so hard, but he had. He thought about her constantly. He hadn't been able to get her out of his mind. But it had taken a near miss for him to realise he had to do something about it. Life was for living and for loving, and if it meant risking being rejected, that was a price he was prepared to pay. He'd tried to run away from his loneliness, but it hadn't worked too well for him, had it? And now that he couldn't run anymore and hiding away in his house with only Biscuit for company wasn't an option, he had to face facts: if he wanted Nora in his life (which he did, more than anything) he'd have to take matters into his own hands.

As Elijah made his way to Nora's house using the bouquet as a foliage shield to hide his face, he had an awful feeling he was about to make the biggest fool of himself ever.

DISMAYED, NORA watched Biscuit pacing around the house. He was doing it again, refusing to settle. It was as though he was searching for something, and as he did circuit after circuit, his ears and tail drooped even more and he began to whine.

Oh, god, was she going to have to take him back? She couldn't bear the thought of him being so miserable. Then again, she was hardly a bundle of joy herself, so he was probably picking up on her frame of mind. Maybe she'd see what he was like tomorrow – give him some time.

Biscuit knew there was someone at the door before the bell even rung. He stiffened and stared into the hall, on full alert. And when the ding-dong chimed, he took a couple of steps forward and woofed, a low warning sound.

'Good boy,' she praised him, pleased his protective side had kicked in. 'Shall we see who it is?' It was probably someone collecting for charity or enquiring whether she needed her gutters cleaning, but when she opened the door, she had the shock of her life as she came face to face with a large bouquet of flowers.

Startled, she stepped back, but she'd forgotten Biscuit was right behind her, and as he pushed past her to greet the newcomer, he took her legs from underneath her.

Nora went down on her bottom with an 'Oof!' and a thud.

Luckily, she still had a significant amount of padding on her backside to cushion her rather ungainly and decidedly inelegant fall, but it still hurt.

'Oh, hell, are you okay?' The beautiful bouquet was cast aside as Elijah hurried to help her up.

Rubbing her behind and hoping she hadn't damaged her coccyx, she said, 'I'm fine. But your flowers aren't.' Yelping enthusiastically, Biscuit was trampling all over them in his haste to greet Elijah as he danced around on his hind legs.

'They're not my flowers, they're yours,' he said, holding out a hand to help her to her feet.

'Mine?' Who from? And why was Elijah delivering them? *Oh!*

'I'm sorry. I was an arse,' he said sheepishly.

'You were. You'd better say hello to Biscuit while I try to rescue the flowers.' About half were salvageable and as she went inside to find a vase to put the poor stems in, she called over her shoulder, 'You'd better come in.'

She heard the door close, and froze, wondering which side of it Elijah might be on.

It was a relief to hear his voice as he tried to calm the excited dog, and when Elijah came into the kitchen, she saw that Biscuit had the hem of his tee shirt in his mouth as though leading him.

Elijah said, 'It's alright, boy, you can let go, I'm not going anywhere. Not yet anyway, not unless your mum kicks me out.'

'Don't temp me,' she growled.

Biscuit, the material still clamped between his teeth, whined uncertainly.

Giving the dog an incredulous look, she said, 'I won't kick him out, okay?' and Biscuit immediately released his hold on the tee shirt, leaving behind a large wet patch.

'Sorry about the flowers,' she said, filling a glass vase with water. 'They're lovely.'

'What's left of them,' he pointed out, despondently.

'It's not Biscuit's fault. He hasn't settled in yet. Still a bit excited. I only brought him home today.'

'He's settled in now.'

So he was. Biscuit was sprawled on the kitchen floor, his nose on his front paws. 'Hallelujah! I was beginning to think he wasn't going to.'

Elijah smiled. 'I've got the magic touch.'

'I hope I haven't got to call on you every five minutes to get him to lie down,' she joked weakly.

'I wouldn't mind if you did.'

Nora sent him a sharp look, which softened when she saw his face. He looked quite forlorn. 'I'm sorry it worked out this way,' she said.

'No, you're not.'

'Okay, I'm not, but I didn't want it to end like this.'

'It doesn't have to end at all.'

'You do realise Biscuit is mine? *I* adopted him.' She prodded herself in the chest.

'I wasn't referring to Biscuit. I was talking about you and me.'

Perplexed, Nora said, 'There isn't a you and me.'

'There could be – if you wanted.'

She narrowed her eyes. 'Is this a ruse to get...?' She stopped, thought about it, then carried on, 'No, it isn't, is it? I mean, it can't be because he's been officially re-homed with me.' She closed her mouth, her thoughts in a tailspin.

Elijah had moved closer.

Slowly, deliberately, he took the flower out of her hand and set it down on the worktop. 'Can I kiss you?' His voice was low and husky.

Lost for words, all Nora could do was nod.

So he did.

And very nice it was too, and when he'd finished kissing her a long, long time later, Biscuit was still lying on the kitchen floor, exactly where they'd left him. The only difference was, the dog appeared to be wearing what could only be described as a self-satisfied grin.

CHAPTER SEVENTEEN

THREE MONTHS LATER

Nora stirred, coming to full wakefulness with a jolt as she realised she was alone in the bed. Her hand crept over to Elijah's side and felt the sheet. It was cold, so he'd been gone a while, she guessed, sitting up.

Where was Biscuit? The dog slept in the bedroom, although he'd remained downstairs when certain activities had taken place last night. But after he'd been let out in the garden to have a wee, Nora had brought him up to bed.

She squinted at her phone, trying to make out the time, and groaned when she realised it was seven thirty-five. She had to leave for the salon in an hour, and she was usually up and about well before now to take Biscuit for his morning walk. Mind you, she and Elijah had been late getting to sleep, and she felt heat sweep up her neck and into her face when she thought of the reason why. They'd been together three months now, and still couldn't get enough of each other, much to Biscuit's disgust. He usually made his displeasure known in the droop of his tail and the accusing look in his eyes whenever he was made to leave the bedroom because they were "busy".

Wondering where the dog was, (Elijah would have left for the bakery hours ago) Nora slipped out of bed and trotted downstairs.

'Biscuit?' she called, before spying him sprawled on the kitchen floor. 'Ah, there you are.' She knelt to give him a cuddle, and he lifted his head and licked her on the nose. 'Sorry, boy, but it's too late to take you for a walk. I've got to go to work. You'll have to make do with the garden.'

Feeling a little cross that Elijah hadn't woken her before he left – he usually did, because he knew how she hated rushing in the morning – she got nimbly to her feet and wondered what she could have for breakfast. But as she flipped the switch on the kettle to make a cup of the herbal tea she'd come to love, a piece of paper lying beside it caught her eye.

Elijah had left a note. How quaint.

I've taken Biscuit for a walk. Breakfast is in the fridge. Yours, not Biscuit's. Thought I'd let you sleep on.

PS. You look really cute when you're asleep.

PPS. You look really cute when you're awake.

PPS. See you later?

NORA HUGGED HERSELF. He certainly *would* see her later. In fact, she'd be most disappointed if he didn't. He'd seen her most evenings since the very first night they'd spent together when he'd brought her flowers after she'd nearly been squished by a car.

Delighted that he'd taken Biscuit out, and that he'd made her some savoury egg muffins for breakfast, Nora tucked into them with relish, thinking once a baker, always a baker, then she had a quick shower, dressed hastily and called Biscuit to her.

The dog rose slowly, yawned and stretched. He looked as languid as she felt, and she wondered how far Elijah had walked him this morning.

She took out her phone. Elijah answered on the third ring.

'Dog walk, then dinner?' she said. 'I'll cook.'

'Do you want me to bring afters?'

'No, *I'm* the afters. Exercise after food is good for my blood glucose,' she told him primly, grinning wider than a Cheshire cat.

'How much exercise are we talking about?'

'That's up to you.' Nora ended the call with a naughty giggle. She was already looking forward to getting home from work and she hadn't even left the house yet!

WHEN NORA AND Biscuit arrived home later that evening, Elijah was waiting for her in her kitchen with a bunch of flowers.

'Do you have something to apologise for?' she asked after he'd greeted the dog (she knew her place in the pecking order).

'Not this time.'

'Then why the flowers?'

'Because I can't bring you chocolates.'

'I don't need chocolates. I don't need flowers, either. All I need is you.'

'And Biscuit,' he pointed out.

'That goes without saying. But why do you feel the need to bring me flowers? I'm not complaining, mind you. Just curious.'

'Because I want to butter you up.'

Elijah took her in his arms and she snuggled into him as he ran his hands down the curve of her waist and over her hips, which were considerably slimmer than when she'd first met him. She'd reached her target weight, was eating healthily with the occasional treat (thanks to Elijah), and was exercising every day (thanks to Biscuit). Her glucose levels, blood pressure, and cholesterol were also all now within normal range – and she intended them to stay that way.

'Why do you want to butter me up?' she asked, nibbling his neck and giggling when he groaned in response.

Biscuit let out a disgruntled huff and turned his back on them. He guessed what was coming next. Nora, however, didn't guess, because what Elijah said came as a complete surprise.

'How do you feel about us moving in together?' he asked.

Nora drew back to look him in the eye. 'I rather like the idea,' she replied, after giving herself a moment to think about it. They were living in each other's pockets most of the time anyway, between her house and his, so it was the sensible thing to do. 'I'm sure can make room for some of your stuff, but not all of it though,' she warned. Her house wasn't all that big.

'What do you mean, "make room for my stuff"? I assumed *you* would move in with *me*.'

'Whatever gave you that idea?' She grabbed his backside and pulled him closer.

'Because I've got a bigger garden.'

'My house is larger, and your garden is only a *bit* bigger than mine,' she countered.

'My kitchen is nicer than yours, and since I do most of the cooking…'

'Only because you're home from work before me. I'm quite happy to cook.'

'You hate cooking!'

'I don't mind it,' she argued.

'Liar.'

He'd got her there; she really wasn't that keen on cooking. 'I've got a power shower,' she pointed out.

'We could have a new one installed in my house.'

'I *like* my house.'

'And I like mine.'

The dog whined and Nora said, 'I've got an idea. We'll ask Biscuit to decide. What do you say, Biscuit?'

Nora and Elijah turned to stare at the dog.

Biscuit had shuffled around to face them and was lying on the floor, his front paws outstretched, panting. He wore an exasperated look on his face, and very slowly he lowered his head and put one paw over his eyes, covering them.

'See!' Nora cried. 'I *told* you he understands every word! God, I *love* that dog.'

'And *I* love *you*.'

Nora froze. The air was suddenly thick, and she tried to catch her breath because his words had knocked the wind out of her.

'You *love* me?' she managed, her voice weak and shaking.

She swallowed hard, her mouth suddenly dry. Her heart was thudding, knocking on her ribs in a staccato rhythm, so loud that she was sure he must be able to hear it.

'I do,' he replied softly.

She bit her lip to stop her chin from trembling. Never in a million years did she think she'd be this happy. Elijah was her world; he'd come into her life when she'd been at her darkest and had lit her up from the inside and taught her how to love – with the help of a certain fluffy hound who was eyeing her with concern, and she realised she was keeping Elijah hanging.

'I love you, too,' Nora murmured. Then kissed him, and it might have gone on for some considerable time if it hadn't been for Biscuit, who squirmed his way in between them and let out a volley of loud barks.

'I think he's telling us he approves,' Elijah said.

Nora beamed. 'How could he not, since it was he who brought us together? Biscuit, you don't mind waiting for your walk, do you?' she asked, and she wasn't in the least bit surprised when he shook his head...

There are loads more large print books in the Muddypuddle Lane series. Available at all good book stores, or ask your local library.

About Etti

Etti Summers is the author of wonderfully romantic fiction with happy ever afters guaranteed.

She is also a wife, a mum, a pink gin enthusiast, a veggie grower and a keen reader.